Intricate Lace

A journey of 3 hearts

Claire Berube

authorHOUSE®

AuthorHouse™
1663 Liberty Drive
Bloomington, IN 47403
www.authorhouse.com
Phone: 1-800-839-8640

First published by AuthorHouse 1/21/2010

ISBN: 978-1-4389-2451-9 (sc)

Library of Congress Control Number: 2008912215

Printed in the United States of America
Bloomington, Indiana

This book is printed on acid-free paper.

PART ONE

Darkness vs Light – "(…) and the truth will set you free."

John 8:32

December 26th

What a stupid Christmas gift! I'm supposed to write stuff in here. Stuff like: I'm fat, I eat too much, and I don't have a boyfriend! What was Mom thinking? Diaries are for babies, not for fifteen-year-olds!

September 15th

Well, who would've thought? Me. Christina Marie Danais! Writing in a dumb diary Mom gave me for Christmas. I had vowed to never write in this but I've got to talk to somebody, if only to a bunch of pages. Have to work at being 'cool' like my new friend says. I can't talk to Mom or Nic about this. Too personal. Too - oh - special I guess. You might be wondering who Nic is? She's a girl I've known since 1st grade. We've been close, but now, not so much. I mean, she's a nerd! She's got fishbowl glasses and she wears these weird clothes her mom makes for her. But, here's the big news! I turned sixteen a week ago and on my birthday I got a surprise!

Charlotte Larin, my new friend, showed me HER diary! Nicole is mad at me 'cause I've been ignoring her, but I don't care! This is tenth grade and I'm entitled to have my choice of friends.

Charlotte's been writing in her diary for the past two years!

She's from St-Joseph's Hall and says that most of the girls there are boarders and they keep a diary because it's the only way they stay sane! She said her parents want her to "experience public high school in French" for a year, so that it will broaden her mind.

I feel so special that she picked me! Nobody else! Me!

It's like she doesn't even mind that I'm overweight. At least I know I'm fat, although she keeps telling me that she likes the *me* inside of me. Mom says as I grow that I'll lose all that 'baby fat'. It's not baby fat, I'm just plain FAT! Fat Angry Teen!

And guess what her parents do? Her mom's a manager for an electronics company and her father is a CEO for a Fortune 500 company! I'm not sure what that means, but they're obviously not short on money like Mom is. She works two jobs.

She's a waitress at the hotel down the road and bartender for weddings and other conferences or something business-like at a hotel close to our house. She walks where she has to go, because we can't afford cabs or taking her car, unless it's an emergency.

Back to Charlotte's parents; they must be loaded with $!!! Charlotte's not even a snob! At least Nic says she is, but I don't think so. She's got the coolest way to describe guys.... you know what she said about Francis? "He's a real hunk and tease...." and then she wiggled her eyebrows up and down. "I wouldn't mind meeting him in a dark stairwell."

And her clothes! I wish Mom would let me wear low-riders, so that I could do like others and get a piercing. Maybe a ruby or diamond? That would be so cool!

Charlotte says that she was at St-Jo's for a couple of years and liked it a lot, but she's mad at her parents for making her move schools. I told her I was happy she had, because I now have a friend and she and I laughed. St-Joseph's Private School is for rich people. Tuition must be in the thousands of dollars. And it's just for girls!

I'm awfully glad Charlotte and I are friends.

Hey! I've just read back what I wrote and it sure is great! Maybe I'll track my fifteenth year, week by week or day by day?

Week by week should be enough.

September 24th

Sure can have lots happen in a week! Mom's looking for a job. Again! You'd think that with two jobs she'd have enough, but she says Christmas is coming and if I've got my heart set on that Jay-Z's Rocawear outfit, she'll need every penny of the new job!

Why do mothers *always* have to exaggerate?

It would save my life! I wouldn't feel so out of place at school. Everyone has at least one item in their closet. Why not me?

Mom keeps telling me she's seen a lot of students that don't at school, but I mean, I want, I *need* to fit in! Sometimes she makes me so mad!

You know what else she says? Charlotte never even went to St-Jo's Hall! How would she know that? So I point blank asked Charlotte and she says my mom was "misinformed".... See? I was right!

Anyway, the two of us went to the mall after school on Friday. I told Mom I was going out with Nicole so she wouldn't get mad at me. She's gotten so paranoid lately that I feel stuck in prison. She's always wanting me to be 'accountable' to her and waiting for her when she comes home from work. Why can Mom go out and work and I can't even be allowed to go to the mall during the week? It's like Mom wants me to stay tied to her 'apron strings', as Charlotte says.

As if I'm hers for eternity! Like I've got no brains or no rights to live my own life by my own rules!

Why does she do that? What can't Mom leave me be just me? Or even trust me?

Plus, she doesn't want me to go out on weeknights to the mall or to the *Dépanneur* or *Gas Stop* or anything when she's not home! I'm like a prisoner chained to the wall!

It's not enough that we live across the street from a police station or that she rents parking to cops! Why didn't she become a cop instead of being a waitress/bartender? All she ever makes me feel is guilty a lot and I feel trapped!

All she wants is for me to come home from school and study, study, study!!!!

What other alternative do I have than to tell her an untruth to escape from this House of Prison? She makes my blood boil!

And to hear her, I'm forgetful and lose stuff all the time. Is it my fault if my house key dropped on the floor and Jerry-The-Bully threw it over the locker, telling me that being I was tall, I could reach over the stack and get it? I had to go to the office and ask the janitors to find my key. They said it wasn't possible, that I'd have to wait until after Spring Break, because they'll have to pull the lockers off the wall to find my key. They suggested I ask Mom for another one.

I had to tell her about the key because when I went to put the spare one in the door, it was crooked and broke in the lock when I tried to take it out!

Charlotte was with me and told me that she had a way to take it out. Well, Mom just about hit the roof when she got home!

What else was I supposed to do? Leave the key in the door? I had to use a nail file to try and get it out, then when that didn't work, I went back to the garage and took a nail and hammer to try to take the half key out.

Now Mom says that she'll need to get a new handle for the back door and match it to the key. Why is she so angry with me? It's not my fault the key broke or that I wasn't suppose to use a nail and hammer! It worked to get the key out, didn't it? At least I got in the house!

Maybe she's got PMS. Charlotte didn't want to stay at our place because she didn't know if Mom would be mad at her for the damage to the door's handle. I told her Mom wasn't like that, but after what happened tonight, I think she's got a point.

September 25th

I was so angry at Mom last night that I forgot to tell you what happened. Charlie (that's what I call her in my mind) and I got to the mall and she showed me how to attract a guy.

There was this really cute security guard and I thought it would be a great challenge, but Charlie said we shouldn't hit on those guys. She said they are always on the lookout for shoplifters and such and don't have time to chat with hot chicks.

OOH! I just realized she called us hot chicks!

We went into this fabulous shop, like, the place where they have designer leather coats and stuff and this guy was so dreamy! I guess he was one of the sales people. Well, she had him eating out of her hand! I could tell he was just waiting to ask her out.

Sitting back and writing about this makes me feel sort of uncomfortable. When I was with her, it was really hard to be a third person in the conversation. I almost felt left out, until she introduced me to him. Mike something or other. I wish he'd asked me out, but I think I'm too fat. Charlie's short and really slim, wears make-up that makes her look older and she wears fashion clothes. I guess I come off as second best or worst best!

She half promised to go out with him.

When we left the mall, she showed me the leather belt she'd bought there last week. It's real leather! She's like - so.... mature and cool! She's got a way of talking and describing people and stores! And she doesn't even look like a fifteen year-old. More like eighteen or twenty.

And you know what? Her mom gave her a credit card! Imagine! A credit card just for her!

She sure spent a lot! (Wish Mom had that kind of money. My life would be *so* much easier to live through.) Charlie bought stuff from electronics to those cool little boas for the Halloween dance at school.

September 26th

I'm grounded for a week! Mom found out that I wasn't with Nicole who called last night. I had to tell her where I was two nights ago as well. There's this weird thing about her eyes that make me say things I want to keep secret! How does she do that?

Now I won't find out if Charlie and Mike go out on their date until tomorrow. Being grounded in my house means, no TV, no stereo, no computer and no phone! How am I going to survive?

Mom says Charlie is a bad influence on me. But she's my friend! She's so much more aware of what goes on around us than Mom is or even Nic. Doesn't she know how hard it is to make friends? I'm fat! Nobody likes fat people! I get teased enough at school! I mean, Jerry-The-Bully-Montcalm bugs me all the time, snatches things off my books and makes my life miserable. Talk about a nasty-watsy guy!

He keeps hiding around corners, waiting, then jumps out, pokes me in the ribs or stomach and says "Pillsbury Dough Girl" and laughs hard and long, his friends as well. Talk about humiliating! I vow now that somehow, somewhere, someday he's going to pay for all of those times!

Charlie keeps telling me that if I just ate chips and pop and not the "good stuff" Mom keeps putting in my lunches and ramming down my throat, that I'd lose weight easily.

Maybe I should try. She also told me about putting a finger down the back of my mouth to make myself throw up. She said that way you eat, but then you don't gain anything, because you throw it all back up again. Sounds simple enough.

But should I try that? Last year in Family Study Class, we looked at eating disorders. Is that anorexia or bulimia? I'll look it up on the Internet at school first before I try it out. Maybe eating less would be better than putting a dirty finger down my throat.

September 28th

Isn't it weird that I said that I was only going to write once a week in here and I'm writing just about every day?

Mom said something really strange this morning while she and I were having breakfast. We were talking about Charlie spending so much money with her credit card. Mom grumbled and mumbled, but I still heard what she said. "Not surprised it still runs in the family."

When I asked her what she meant, she just took a sip of her coffee and suggested I make sure she's spending her own money and not someone else's.

Like whose? Her mom or dad's? After all, they gave her her own credit card. Why wouldn't she use it?

September 29th

I guess Mom's got a point. Today Charlie dropped her purse and two credit cards popped out. I couldn't help but notice that one of them didn't have her name on it. She just shrugged her shoulders and said that it was her mom's.

I thought her mom's name was Bernadette? The card said Roxanne Shulter and the other C. Meanning. I asked her why and she said her mom used her middle name and maiden name on the card and that the other was one she found on the ground. She said she had to return it to the bank today.

I told her she could just drop it off at the police station across the street from my place on her way home. She turned back into her locker and said that her mom had suggested the bank.

I wonder about that.... where did she find that extra card and why would she say that she had to bring it only to that bank? Wouldn't any bank do? Or even better the cops?

September 30th

Last night before I fell asleep, my mind kept going around in circles about those credit cards and I hope that they aren't stolen. Maybe Charlie collects old credit cards. It would certainly explain what I found in her purse. During Gym class today, I had to go change a pad real bad, so I asked to be excused. Charlie was on the ropes and she was busy making eyes at Francis, so I figured she wouldn't find out what I was going to do after I changed my pad.

It isn't just one card, it's six! And they're all different companies and all have different names and numbers! What if she stole them? Or her Mom?

But she's my friend! I trust her! We have fun together, and we're best friends!

She wouldn't do that! Would she?

I almost got caught in the locker room. Thank goodness my locker is right next to hers. Nicole came in and gave me this weird look. Like a sad one. She's such a loser! Can't she see that she won't be able to find a guy if she doesn't stop looking like a wet rag?

Maybe I should wait and see what Charlie says about the cards. Maybe I'm wrong. Maybe I dreamt seeing them. Maybe Nic looked sad because we're no longer friends.

October 1st

Mom okayed the library for Saturday but put down a curfew of noon, so I've got just enough time to get ready tomorrow morning. I said that Joanne and I were going because we have this project to work on for Geography class. We're to meet at ten. Well, it's true; we do have a project together, except we're already finished.

I didn't want to talk to Mom about all those credit cards and I feel kind of silly asking Charlie. What if she's collecting them from the aunts and uncles in her family? The last thing I want is for her to get angry and drop me as a friend.

October 2nd

Charlie and I snuck out of the library as planned and headed for the mall next door. I like that there are different branches of the city library. I still get to be on the safe side for Mom and still go malling with Charlie.

Because it's our 1 month anniversary of meeting, Charlie gave me a small gift.... *Aubergine* nail polish and a butterfly pin with what looks like diamonds, but I know they're just rhinestones because she wouldn't spend money on diamonds for me. It's about 2 inches high and it shines a lot! It's really pretty!

I came home at noon just like I promised and because it was Mom's morning off, she asked how our project went. I told her it was okay. Last time I didn't hand in a project paper, Mr. Boissonneault about blew his top and asked me if I wanted to fail tenth grade! I don't want to fail tenth, just get by. That's enough, isn't it? On top of that, he called Mom and she had to come to school and promise to make me work harder at my homework projects. This time, Joanne and I finished our work at school. That way nobody will complain and I won't have Mom on my back again.

October 3rd

Mom had to do a double shift today at the hotel, so I invited Charlie over to help pass the time. We had a party!

We tried some of Mom's more outrageous outfits as well as some of the historical dresses she borrowed from one of her friends to copy. Mom has a friend who sews and does historical re-enactment fairs. They get all dressed up in the dresses of the period and walk around the land for weekends and cook and do weird dances on the Saturday night and so on. I used to like doing that with her, but not any more. I think it's too babyish.

Charlie and I laughed a lot. I had to go hunt in Mom's jewelry box for the pearl choker she always wears with the red Flapper dress of the dirty thirties. Charlotte looked like it was made for her. Her hair style is even just right!

October 9th

So much has happened in the last week that I don't know where to start!

Mom found out about the butterfly pin when I wore it on Sunday for church. I told her Charlie had given it to me and she asked me when. That's when I started feeling as if she was trying to make me tell her something she already knew. I didn't want to tell her of the day we went to the library, so I told her the day we went to the mall.

Mom did this weird twisty thing with her lips that she does when she's not too happy with me and told me that it was too flashy for church. She said to leave it at home, that she'd have a look at it later. I wondered why at the time, but now, it's sort of weird.

When we came back from church, our side door was unlocked and open. Mom swears we locked it and it's true that she always does.

We got broken in!

All of Mom's gold jewelry is missing! So is the painting that used to hang in the living room, our stereo equipment and an opal ring that was probably worth more than any other piece of jewelry in her box! Mom is very upset. She called the cops and they did a report and told her to call her insurance company.

What I can't understand is why they would ask me if I knew of anyone who would know about the contents of Mom's jewelry box! It's almost like they know something, but they aren't telling anyone! Why do I feel guilty when I don't know anything?

October 11th

Charlie wasn't at school today. I wonder if she's sick. I tried to call her at home at lunch, but there was no answer. Not even the answering machine. Maybe she's out of town?

October 12th

Her grandmother died and she had to go to the funeral yesterday. She says she's tired of school and can't wait for this semester to be over.

Charlie's acting kind of weird today, but maybe it's because she's tired and sad. I'll get her some chocolate covered almonds. Those are her favorite pick-me-ups. Maybe it'll cheer her up.

October 14th

Mom's new job at the pub downtown finishes at five. She works there every Monday and Thursday. She's not usually back until six, so that gives me about two hours after school to do homework. But who wants to do that when I can go out with Charlie to the malls?

We got to Tuxedo Mall tonight. Charlie bought some perfume and when we went through the expensive jewelry counter, she saw a gorgeous diamond and emerald necklace.

She asked the attendant to see it and it really is beautiful up close. Would you know? It's worth three thousand dollars!!!! The attendant asked if Charlie wanted to try it on, but she said maybe I'd like to try it.

I felt like a princess and the necklace felt cool and heavy next to my throat and I wished that my hair was up in curls and ringlets and I saw myself wearing this really long dress and having this cute guy next to me, then asking me to dance. I kind of hit the ground when the salesgirl asked me to give it back. I couldn't undo the clasp at the back, so Charlie offered to help me, but the salesgirl said she'd do it. She put it back and Charlie and I stayed a while longer just to look at the other necklaces on display.

Wish I could afford things like that! Maybe one day..... *when* my prince comes.

We had lots of fun after that. We stopped at the cosmetics counter and tried different shades of nail polish, and perfume. Then we hopped on the bus and I made it home and into my room just in time for Mom to come home.

Except she snapped her cap! She bawled me out because I didn't do the dishes or answer the phone when she called me earlier!

Why do parents *always* give us the garbage jobs to do?

October 24th

Charlie's a stinking liar!!!!

I kept wondering why she and I never went to the same mall twice.

Now I know.

I should have listened to Mom and Nic!

At least I've learnt my lesson! It's going to take more than smiles and a jewelry pin before I listen to HER again!

She makes me MAD! MAD! MAD!

She actually turned against me at the mall and Mom had to come and bail me out. I think I'm going to die of shame!

Me! Caught shoplifting! Ugh!

Charlie slipped the pearl and diamond necklace in my pocket without me noticing! Why didn't I see it coming? She kept telling me that we could do whatever we wanted to do, out with the old and in with the new. That no one would see us doing anything wrong! Liar!

Remember the emerald necklace and when she wanted to take it off me and the salesgirl did instead? This time Charlie tricked the sales person into believing that another customer was looking for another necklace. When she stepped away from us, Charlie went behind me and took off the necklace and then slipped it in my pocket without me noticing and when they searched her at the store, she was clean and because I was with her, I was searched too!

I'm innocent! Charlie looked at me as if I was a snake under a rock! Like it was my fault? She said she didn't know that I was a shoplifter and she and I were done!

Then she turned away from me when I called to her and you know what she said?

"Why should I care about you? You're the one caught shoplifting, not me!"

"I never put *that* in my pocket! Why are you blaming me? You and I are best friends! You said that you liked me."

She shook her head and hissed back: "Friends? You're out of your mind! You're so fat, you're dumb!"

She was so cruel! How can she say that when she's told me over and over that she liked me a bit overweight and plump? I almost expected to be hauled off by cops, but the store security people wouldn't let Charlie and I go. I really wanted Charlie to fess up to putting that necklace in my pocket, but she kept repeating that she'd never touched it!

Mom was even less impressed. She had to come and get me at the store.

Sigh! We were brought to the offices of the store upstairs by the security guards. There, Charlie and I were asked to sit down in front of this man behind a desk. All I remember is shaking like a leaf and sweating like crazy.

The man at the desk asked me for my father's name and phone number. I told him I didn't have one and he could call my mom. Then he turned to Charlie and his eyes were cold like ice. He said something really weird then. He said that they had had their eye on her from the moment she stepped into the store!

The security camera caught Charlie not only stealing the necklace, but also a brooch and other stuff for the last two weeks. The security guards didn't just happen to stop us from leaving the store. The sales person called them with a buzzer they have next to the counters.

Do you know that the butterfly pin was from that store too? And she stole them! And then she denied that she'd done any of it! Blamed me for goading her to a dare! Liar!

They (the security people) caught her on camera! Not just once, but three times!

How can she deny that she didn't do it? The man behind the desk replayed the security tape and I saw what happened! It was there in black and white that she took the necklace and when she realized she was being watched, bumped into me, slipped her hand into my pocket and dropped it!

I'm probably going to have to witness against her in court! She's so........aaaaaargh!!!!

The cops arrested her and took her away. Mom came and asked the security man what I was going to have to do.

The man looked at me and asked me what I thought I should do. I swallowed really hard and said that I was going to be a lot more careful in choosing my friends from now on. He said it was a good start then asked if there was anything else.

I said I'd be praying to God a lot more and that I was done with Charlie! I also told him I didn't really like jewelry and that I'd learnt my lesson. Handcuffs weren't ever going to be for me again! Mom kind of choked and then coughed and the man's eyes smiled at me. He said I was on the right track.

At least Mom didn't say much on the ride back. She's pretty smart. The bus isn't really a good place for a private conversation. She and I sat up late tonight to talk it over. I asked her to forgive me for acting so stupid and being so obnoxious to her. I wonder now if she'll ever get her pieces of jewelry back. I talked to Mom about it and she said:

"Even if I don't get anything back, I've got the daughter of my heart right here. My Teena isn't going to jail and she's going to be a better person because of this experience."

One thing I'm learning. If a person tells me something that I believe isn't true about me, I'll remember Charlie and remind myself of what happened today.

October 25th

It's really tough when you live right across the street from a cop shop! Every time I go out the door now, I feel guilty! Mom says I'd better get used to it. It's what's going to keep me on the straight and narrow road.

It used to make me feel real safe. Terry and John park out back every week and Jay on the alternate shift. Every time I see them now, I feel like they know all about me! About my 'almost-arrest'. Except it wasn't my fault!

All I wanted was a friend! All I wanted was to be accepted as one of the crowd! Why couldn't Charlie have been more like.... like Nicole? Oooh, Nic..... I hope she can forgive me.

You know, Diary, I've just read back over yesterday's entry and there's a question here. I wonder if Charlie was responsible for the break-in we had a few weeks ago?

The butterfly pin did disappear and she was with me when I lost my key at school and had to get the spare one out of the garage. And-- I just thought of something else!

She said she had a friend who was a painter. What if he took the painting? What if she only pretended to like me as a friend so she could use me for bait? Maybe she bribed Jerry to toss my key over the lockers on purpose?

What if she tricked me into playing dress up so she could see if Mom and I had good enough jewelry to sell? Mom didn't change our hiding place for the spare keys. It would have been a piece of cake for Charlie to find it. Dang! I'd better tell that to Mom. Now I'm pretty sure it was her!

Charlotte Larin is no longer my friend. She's shown me her true colors. She's a chronic mean, scheming, cheating liar! Never am I going to be caught like this again.

October 27th

I think I'm recovering. That's what Mom says. She says there's some lessons in life that she can't teach me, that I have to learn them on my own.

I wonder how she knows all this stuff. She's 38 and sometimes - well, a lot of times - we don't see eye to eye. There are other times we're like two pieces of gum!

And I can forget the Jay-Z's Rocawear for Christmas and going to the Halloween dance at school. I'm grounded! Maybe for the rest of the year, who's to know? I know I really screwed up. It's going to be a long time before I go malling again. I'm never going to lie to Mom again!

October 30th

Want to hear something? Charlie got kicked out of school! I guess she's been lying all along.

Mom was right! She didn't go to St-Jo's Hall. It was all a ploy, a lie that she wanted me to believe so that I'd think she was rich.

Why do people do that? Am I that gullible? I believe everything people tell me! Mom says that I'm always looking for the best in people and she says I wear 'blinders' in front of my eyes instead of looking at the flaws too. I guess I should talk to God and ask Him to cure me of that trait.

At least there's a consolation - I won't have HER looking at me all the time making me feel about an inch high. I wonder why she got kicked out though. Maybe Mr. Prevost heard about the jewelry store. I wonder......

Mom said that I should look on the bright side of the lesson. I asked her what she meant. "What did you learn from this?" So here are my answers:

- I know that next time I'll choose my friends so that they won't be like Charlie. If we go malling again, I'll make sure I don't buy anything out of my money range. (And I'm not ever getting a credit card! It's obvious to me now that the credit cards in her purse were stolen.)

- Smiles and promises of lots of fun didn't work for me. Next time I'll wait before I trust someone else.

- Shoplifting is against the law and it's something I'll never forget as long as I live!

Then Mom said something that made me see that she knows I've been writing in this diary. "Writing about our feelings on paper helps a lot. Try it and see."

I wonder if she's got a diary. If she does, it must be really huge!

November 11th

Day off school. Remembrance Day. Thank God! I hate that day, because in the past we had to drill to "O Canada" and something called "Taps" that the school's best trumpet player got to play while the flag rises up the pole in front of the school.

Mr. Schoenberg (he's my English teacher) said that his dad got shrapnel in his knee and he's never recovered from being in a concentration camp.

There are wars all over the world! It's interesting that Canadians are called in as peace keepers. Blue Berets I think they call them.

Mr. S. said that his father also suffers from something called "war memory stress syndrome". This is when soldiers witness barbaric human cruelty. They often have nightmares for a long time.

Yesterday, we had the visit of three soldiers that did a round of duty in Afghanistan. They came to speak to the school.

I never knew that being a soldier wasn't just about standing at attention and fighting. It's a lot more! They showed us some pictures from the country in which they were. There's one that really impressed me.

There were these houses that looked really nice. Nice gardens in front and children playing in the street. Then they ran a video clip of a newscast. I don't think I want to be a soldier or even join the military.

After the bombs fell, there were children lying in the streets, not moving. Not even breathing! The houses were not even there! What if there had been people in them?

Our soldiers said that they were showing us these clips and pictures to tell us something. I wanted to throw up! Those poor kids! I don't want to see those pictures again for a very long time.

I've got good news though! Nic is going steady with Stéphane and Gil is going steady with Pawly Wally. Mom says they're too young, but I don't think so. It's a relief to go to dances and not have to be left standing against the wall or worse, sitting alone at your table.

I overheard two teachers talking about Charlie today. She got kicked out because she stole some school records and money. How could I have believed her? How could I have been so blind to the obvious! Like why did I believer her story about the credit cards?

I'm not going to be suckered in again. I'm not going to be stupid like that either. It's going to be different from now on!

September 30th

It's been almost a year since I've last written in here. That's because I wanted to finish tenth grade on a good note; especially since it wasn't a good beginning. I see this as being something to help me keep a record of what I can accomplish in school this year. I'm now in another home class and I like my home room teacher.

October 10th

Remember Mr. Schoenberg? He died in a car accident. Most of the school was upset. He was a tough teacher, but we sure learnt a lot from him. This year he's been replaced by this awesome teacher. She's a cool dresser and most of us are all taller than she is. But she also knows how to handle the guys.

They can't get over the fact that she knows when they're up to playing a trick on her and she just laughs and says that she could see it coming.

Mrs. Bibeau is her name and she's really nice. The guys tease her a lot, but she told us she comes from a big family. Imagine having 8 brothers! *And* being the only girl! I wonder how she survived. I'm an only child and sometimes I feel as if having a sister or brother would drive me up the wall!

Friends are friends because we choose them, but bros and sis? Woah!

Nic and Steph broke up this August. She's now going steady with André and it seems to be going okay with her. We're back as friends and she forgave me over Charlie.

She said she understood that sometimes we don't see the worst in people. She said I'm always blind in that department and I guess she's right. I always try to see the best in people. Why shouldn't I? Mom is always telling me that I need to look deeper than the outer package.

But I can see Nic's point. If I had used my eyes and common sense, I would have seen that Charlie's many credit cards were stolen ones. It also explains why she insisted the bank was the best option. I'm sure now that she has a criminal record, otherwise, why would she have refused to give the cards to the police station?

October 21st

There's a new program in the Family Life Course. It's called Baby Think It Over, where we have to take an electronic plastic-rubber baby doll home with us for twenty-four hours on the first part of the course, and then forty eight on the second one.

Mrs. Dandeneau, our school counselor says that we also have the option of a week.

Inside the doll, there's an electronic memory chip that makes it act like a real newborn baby. I think that's so cool! I like babies. They're so soft and cuddly.

It even cries and wets its diaper like a real kid! Mom said that I needed to take this course because it would help me understand what it's like to be a single parent.

When Mom was 22 she was pregnant with me. She said that the first few months of her pregnancy, she had a lot of morning sickness. Sometimes I feel like I don't have a father because Mom never mentions him. Maybe he died before I was born?

Every time I bring up the subject, Mom refuses to talk to me about it. It's so frustrating! I just want to know who he is! Instead she reminds me I'm her daughter and that's all that matters.

October 22nd

Mrs. D is teaching the Baby course. She asked me if I knew Rosanne Danais and when I said she was my mom, she asked if I knew Roger Danais, Sr. of Riverton. I said no. She frowned and said: "Oh," and switched to another student.

I guess she doesn't know that Mom's never told me.

So, I came home and asked Mom tonight. She sat down real quick at the kitchen table and just stared at me. It was really eerie for a minute and then I knew that Mrs. D. had been right. Mom does have relatives!

I asked Mom why she'd never told me!

She cleared her throat then said that her family and she don't get along and that they turned their backs on her when she got pregnant with me. She said she lost their respect and hasn't talked to them in years.

So what's wrong with trying to find them now, I asked her? Do they know I even exist? Do my grandparents even realize they have a granddaughter?

She started crying and then said that what was important was that I was loved by someone who would always be there for me.

I don't think that's an answer and I'm going to try to find out for myself! Maybe I can ask Mrs. D and go from there. It's going to be tough not letting Mom know about this, but I *need* to know where I come from!

October 24th

Mom caught on to what I was trying to find out. She gave me the silent treatment this morning. What's with her?

I mean, I really, REALLY want to know!

November 1st

Mom's thawed a bit, but she says that she doesn't have time to talk about it right now. Like when?

November 8th

In Family Life class, I learned how to change a diaper, like I didn't do enough baby-sitting at the neighbours! But it's okay I suppose. Mrs. D says even if we've already done that, it's always a good thing to have a refresher. See with the electronic babies we've got to be as consciencious, no - that should be 'tious'. (That looks weird! Maybe scious?) I'll have to check the dictionary in a bit.

So.... we need to be careful. These "babies" are really sensitive to everything we do to and with them.

November 15th

I've got this "baby" here. His name is Paul Blue. It won't stop crying! I'm holding it in my arms and rocking it. I've tried everything it says in the book. I've changed the diaper, fed him, talked to him and now I'm holding him, in fact, bouncing him would be a better word. What have I forgotten?

I tried to get some info from Mrs. D about Mom's parents and family, but she said to ask Mom. It's not fair! Mom won't even talk about it!

How can I figure it out if she won't talk to me?

November 16th

Mrs. Dandeneau says that we need to remember to "burp" our babies after we feed them, otherwise they get air trapped in their stomachs and that causes them to have upset tummies. She said it was like us when we've eaten too much. If we don't let some air out, we can't get our stomachs to settle down. She says babies don't have the 'burp reflex', they have to learn that.

That's what I forgot to do!

November 17th

It's 2 a.m.! I wonder how Mom could ever have done this. This doll is driving me crazy! Every time I put the carrier down, he cries! Every time I feed him, he screams! Every time I change his diaper, he reacts! What am I doing wrong?

3:30 a.m. I've been holding this doll, singing to it for the past half-hour. He's finally dropped off. I never want to have a baby in my life!

4:55 a.m. He's awake again! I've changed his diaper and am now feeding him a bottle. When will this night end?

7:30 a.m. I have to write everything that I do in a journal. The only thing is, I can't seem to be able to keep my eyes open long enough to write what I have to write. Thank goodness I don't have to pretend in this one.

In the journal, I just have to say what I do for the doll. Here I can spew off my feelings all I want!

Mrs. D said that we will get these babies again in a month for forty eight hours and that if we don't go along with this plan, that we flunk the class.

Talk about blackmail though! I need this course for a credit this year. I can't fail!

November 19th

Phew! Am I glad I've got a month to catch up on my sleep! Twenty four hours was long enough, thank you very much! Nicole is now the one that's got my doll for the next weekend. Hope she has better luck!

I wonder if Mom went through this with me. I asked her and she said that although it was tough and a challenge, she was glad because she's got a great daughter now.

Sometimes she says the nicest things!

November 23rd

You remember I was looking for my extended family? Well, turns out they're from a small village, just south east of the city, mostly grain and dairy farmers. But I wasn't able to find out much.

There are three Danais in the town directory. I wanted to call, but what if they hang up on me?

What can I say? "Hi, I'm Christina Danais. I'm the daughter of Rosanne Danais. Could you tell me if my father is still alive?"

That would probably shock them or worse, they could hang up on me. Maybe I should wait until Mom is ready to tell me. Hopefully it will be soon.

Or never!

December 8th

Well, today I start a weekend-long trial with the "Thing". I have to take it everywhere I go. Do you know that includes the bathroom? And shower? And my bedroom and church?

For the whole weekend and up to Tuesday morning!

December 9th - 4 a.m.

How could anyone do this? I've been up twice already and frankly I am in no mood for jokes.

Mom just smiled and she's not saying anything, but I know what she's thinking...... *better get used to it, kiddo.* I think I'm going to wait to have kids.

Did you know parents are told *not* to get involved?

December 10th

In church, would you believe this baby starts bawling in the middle of the message? And he was so loud, that the pastor asked me to leave the room because they were filming? Talk about embarrassing!

Never mind Paul Blue - I've got a name for this baby - Monster.

He's a monster all right! He's just plain hungry all the time! It's 3 a.m. and the doll is on his third bottle of the night!

I've had maybe one hour of sleep and tomorrow I've got a semester final exam for math. (Not one of my better subjects.)

December 11th

In the middle of the exam, Monster started whimpering and I had to pick him up and hold him against my shoulder while I was writing it. How come I'm the only one that's got a bawling kid?

Nic says that Monster didn't do this for her. Maybe it's me.

Maybe I'm not cut out for the "Mom" thing. Maybe having kids is for later. I found myself screaming at the thing when I came home from school and I wanted to throw the doll against the wall! I hope the memory doesn't pick up on that! I am *so* frustrated with this doll it's not even funny! I am *not ever* going to be a mother.

I wanted to go shopping tonight after class for Christmas presents and I did start out, but Monster got in the way.

He started screaming his little head off as soon as he got on the bus. I couldn't shut him up! So I had to get off the bus and walk back home. HE cried ALL the way home! What is wrong with this mutt?

Can't wait to get him off my hands tomorrow morning. Mrs. D is going to get a piece of my mind.

December 12th

Would you believe it? Mrs. D is sick and the counselor, who took her course load, said that we have to keep our "kids" until she comes back! I begged her to let me hand him in, but she said that she had no idea how the dolls work and that the director had instructed her to tell the students what they were expected to do.

It's a plot, I just know it......

Talk about turning us off parenthood...... I don't know how anyone could do this. Even the guys in this course have it easy. Why am I the one that's got a doll with the mouthiest memory?

For the past two nights I've hardly slept! Monster is awake every hour and a half! I change him; cuddle him and just plain hold him in my arms all day! I pace at night and even during class!

I can't go anywhere anymore!

It's like I live in a prison! And I thought being grounded was bad! Being grounded by a baby is a hundred times worse! I wish I could put this doll in the garage and leave him there until the end of the week comes!

If only I could tell Mrs. D that I want out of this now! But I've got to hang on until she's back. I need this course's notes to pass my year. Whoever thought this course was easy needs to have his head examined!

December 14th

Someone mentioned that they think Mrs. D should be back tomorrow. I sure hope so! Last night of this nightmare! I can't wait!

Today I fell asleep in Chemistry class and Mr. Rémillard had to shake me awake. He looked at me with sympathy, (I think), and reminded me that a bed was more comfortable than the edge of the counter and that he preferred his students to be awake during his classes.

I told him about the baby doll keeping me awake at night and he smiled. He's a real sweetheart. He's the proud father of triplets. He says that he's glad that we all have the opportunity to take care of the babies in the Think-It-Over program, because it gives us a good insight on the reality of parenthood.

Nic said that André was not impressed with the fact that they had to take the baby with them to the movies last time she had Monster. But at least he didn't cry for her during that time.

How does she do it? I passed her my doll just to see what she did different from me and he quieted right down in her arms! What am I doing wrong? As soon as I took him into mine he started fussing again and then he started to cry!

Nic can't explain it more than I can. If I ever have children, I'd better have a nanny. I'm never going to be able to handle a baby if he acts like this all the time.

I tested out Teena's Theory later at break time. I asked Ronnie (her real name is Veronique) if I could hold her baby and she said: "Why? You think it's just because mine cries too that you'll be able to keep it quiet? Think we should switch babies or something?"

"Why not?" I said, "Maybe your doll would be quieter than mine."

So we tried. No such luck! Her doll started screaming at the top of her lungs and Monster went quiet in her arms! Guess what? I'm not surprised! My theory says that I'm not good with babies, that I'm not mother material. I'm never going to have babies, never going to get pregnant! I'll stay single and have no fear of having to look after them.

December 15th

I went to the supermarket with Mom tonight and Monster was quiet for the first time since I've had him! I got my learners permit so I drove. Mom says I'm a very good driver.

But, all hell broke loose when we were in the car coming back!

He wouldn't feed, wouldn't respond to singing or music from the radio (and I tried different stations, even classical!) and I couldn't stop the car on the highway to look after him! His screams were driving me nuts!

Now I know I'm going to flunk this course! Mom didn't even help! And I couldn't do anything either! I was driving and at the first stop we came to, I turned to her and said:

"I am not ever going to have kids even when I'm old and gray! Right now, I just want to take Monster and throw him out the window!"

She put her arm around me and said: "Teena sweetheart, every mother feels the way you do at one time or another when she has a baby to look after. It's part of being a parent. It doesn't mean we love our child less. Don't be so hard on yourself. You'll get the hang of it soon."

Hang of it? I've had this doll for close to a week now and I'm still having the same problems! How would she know? She was older when she had me! I hate this baby! Hate being stuck with a kid! I know I'll be a rotten mother! I'm not such a fool that I would jeopardize my studies with getting pregnant! I want to be a dentist later, so that means no sex for at least ten years after I graduate!

I'm hoping that by then, I'll be more mature and more in control of my emotions.

We got home and I picked Monster up and he stopped crying right away. I changed his sopping wet diaper (crying does make him pee more), cuddled him some more and then he went to sleep and I crashed on my bed.

Fact is he woke up a half-hour later screaming again! I am never, never, NEVER, going to have babies!

December 16th (Saturday)

Rumors are rumors. Mrs. D isn't going to be back until next week!

How am I going to hang on? As it is, I haven't had a single night of more than half hour snoozes. Every time I look in the mirror, the rings under my eyes are getting bigger and bigger. And I'm so tired now that I feel like crying all the time!

December 18th

I've never been as happy as when I handed Monster over to Mrs. Dandeneau with my journal. I told her about the last few nights and the fact that I'm so tired now, that I don't know if I'll ever be able to sleep more than half an hour at a time, I'm so into that routine! I also told her that I fell asleep in Chem. class and she chuckled and said that Mr. Remillard had told her.

I told her about our drive on the highway and how it was really tough having this kid. She said she understood and that she wasn't the one who made the electronic memories for each baby.

She asked me if I had had a chance to come up with a nickname for him. (That was one thing that happened with the other people in my class.... they called their babies 'peanut', 'minou' - which is kitten in French, and so on) I told her bluntly that it was Monster. She was horrified! Then she burst out laughing and said: "As bad as that?"

I said yes and added that I was never going to have children. Not even if I have a career and a husband!

She just smiled at me and winked.

December 19th

Thank goodness today is an in-service day. You know what? It's eight thirty at night and I've been asleep since 6 last night! Having a baby is way too tiring for me. At least Mrs. D said that I passed and Mom was a real sweetheart. She let me sleep and bought me a pink rose and a cuddly teddy bear! She said I could hug it and it didn't have a memory or anything to remind me of the doll.

December 21st

At last Christmas holidays! I learnt something during the Baby-Think-It-Over course.

I noticed that when Mom held him, he'd quiet right down, but when I held him, he screamed! Same thing happened with Ronnie. And Nic – she's more like Mom.

I guess I'm too impatient. I like to have things done quickly so I don't have to do them over again.

Looking after a baby, you're always doing the same things: change, feed, cuddle, sing.... change, feed, cuddle, sing, rock..... See what I mean? B-O-R-I-N-G!

I will never be a mother! Never! Never! NEVER! I'm going to be a terrible influence on a child too! Remember how much I yelled and wanted to throw the doll to shut him up? I'd probably yell at the kid like I did Monster. That's not a good thing to do with kids.

If there's one thing I've learnt with this course is just that: I won't - can't be a mother. I can love other people and adults, but children and babies are not going to be part of my life.

March 18th

I haven't written in a while, but I need to talk to something before I burst! You know who I'm going steady with?

Harry Slocombe!

Talk about a dream come true! He is soooooo awesome! He's got gorgeous gray eyes! Silver and light and shimmery. I just melt every time he looks at me. I feel all warm inside, like I'm floating.

And when he touches my hand, I walk on air. He's got this so cool smile. Makes my knees knock.

Mom says that she doesn't mind me going steady, now that I'm seventeen, but to keep it simple and not to go out with him on my own, to always be in a group!

She's so old-fashioned! Harry is real handsome, even in jeans and muscle shirt. And he's got these real strong biceps and six-pack abs. He's really fit. He works out at the gym three times a week.

He's a little older than me. He doubled fifth and eighth grade, but he's also working. He's a transfer student from Tec Voc where he's learning machining.

We don't have that course at CLR Collegiate, so he's taking the French courses for an extra credit. His mom is French and he says it's important to master at least two languages. I asked him why he didn't pick Spanish and he just shrugged his shoulders. Said he already tried that but he didn't like it.

March 20th

Harry and I, Nic and André went out for fries and had a good time! It's amazing that I feel so comfortable with him. Remember Charlie? She was from another school too and yet, with Harry, it's like he's so much more mature and trustworthy than she was. Or maybe, like he says, I'm mature for my age.

He's got two jobs. He's a driver for a rich family and he also works in a restaurant.

March 21st

Harry gave me the nicest shirt ever! See, it's close to my birthday, so he said it was "just because". He's into 'ying, yang' stuff, and it's real cool listening to how our lives have this pull from Ying to Yang. And it makes sense. More than what Mom keeps telling me about God. How can God know that some days I'm feeling good? Or bad, for that matter. I'm just one person out of billions to him.

I was talking about my new blouse. It's clear, well, sort of.... Harry called it "opaque", which he says is the "in" thing right now. I bet he paid lots for it. As a chauffeur, he makes a lot of tips. I saw the long limo he drives. It's more like the 'party limos' I see a lot of during the weekends. He says that he'll let me ride with him soon, if his boss lets him. During the week, he works two evenings at the restaurant as a—he called it a special name....mitro dee, or something like it. He takes people to their tables.

He's real smart! He's at my school because he wants to add credits to his grade 12 so that he can enter university to become a lawyer. Because he works for that rich family, he said we might go out together on the nights he doesn't work. Like later this week.

He said to get all dressed up on Thursday because he wants to take me out on the town, but Mom said to wait until we know each other better.

I guess that's maybe a good idea.... I don't want Harry to get any ideas that I'm too willing to be with him. Nicole always says that it's better to play hard to get, than to play 'I'm here waiting.'

March 22nd

I looked up the word "opaque" in the dictionary today. It says it's a thick, difficulty seeing through type of thing, like fabric or fog. I told Harry that the dictionary said it was diaphanous.

He got real mad and yelled at me saying that I had to go and ask someone else instead of him, that I didn't trust him. I said that it wasn't that I didn't trust him, just that: "I think my blouse is 'sheer'."

His eyes turned steely gray, almost black and I got scared when he grabbed my arm. It hurt! I tried to yank it from him, but he twisted it then leaned across me and opened my door.

"I think it'd be a better idea if you went in your house now before I do something I'll not be proud of. "

What's with him? It was just a word! Not like I attacked him or anything. That was so weird! He's never gotten this angry before. I think... no, I *do* love him. He's so cool and cute and nice.... well, most of the time. I guess every relationship has its ups and downs. Maybe he had a bad day at work.

He almost scared me as much as Charlie did, but she never hurt me like that. I thought he was so nice. Have I made a mistake? Is he going to break off with me because of this? Why is it that I have so many problems trusting friends? It's like I'm always looking for recognition.... no that's not it. I know! Affection!

Yeah, that's what it is. Harry is really affectionate. At least he usually is. I mean, we hold hands and he puts his arm around my shoulder when we walk together. Isn't that what going steady is all about? I wish I had a dad. I could ask him what makes guys tick.

Not that Mom isn't the greatest, but she doesn't seem to like Harry. She only met him once, so how can she judge him just by what he wears? A lot of guys wear leather pants. Why can't my boyfriend wear them too?

Mom says that he's got the 'bad boy' look all over him. She said the same thing about Charlie. But Harry is different! He's a real gentleman. I'm sure he loves me.

I'm sure he'll call. I hope.

March 24th

Guess what I got today? A dozen red roses!!!! And a little teddy bear. And a card with a broken heart on it! There's only one word in it: Sorry. Isn't that sweet? Now I know he loves me. Harry will be changing from now on. I'm sure now that he won't scare me like that again.

March 25th

You know what? I've lost fifteen pounds these past two months. What a difference! Harry says he like the new me lots more than the old one. He says that this success deserves a special celebration, but before that, I've got eight more pounds to lose.

Mom says that I'm really taking charge of my body and that she likes this new me, but to remember that it's not good to lose too much weight and not get any ideas that I'm not thin enough. She says that could cause me to get anorexia.

She said it's a disease that makes you believe you're never thin enough and can actually cause someone to die.

Woah! I mean, die? She said that sometimes a person's heart gets so weak that it stops beating. I'm going to be real careful from now on..... I don't want to be so skinny that I'll disappear.

Remember when Charlie and I were friends? She was talking about bulimia and I looked it up on the Internet. I guess anorexia nervosa is the same thing, except you don't eat. You get the same results..... a nervous breakdown and a ruined life.

Not for me.

March 28th

This is just for your ears and paper.... I was kissed for the first time by Harry! Nic used to tell me that she saw stars when all her boyfriends kissed her.... she's in the bean field! When Harry and I kiss, it's like a home run! Like the crack when the ball hits the bat.

I just explode inside. Harry is soooo good at it too. And he said that all the girls like to be petted, because it helps us get more into the kiss. I *know* he loves me. I even think that he had a crush on me before we even met face to face.

It felt so exciting to be touched under my jacket. But when he got too close to my private parts, I just said no, and he didn't go any further. He respects me.

April 1st

So far, I've lost thirty pounds. Mom is starting to worry that I'm losing too much too fast, but I've told her that I'm stopping dieting now. I'm back to eating a burger a week and having some bits of cookies and I cheated today and had a huge bowl of ice cream. Mmmm! Good stuff!

April 15th

Mom doesn't know this. Harry took me to a bar. I'm not yet 18, but he said I look older when I wear makeup. I blended right in! The bouncers didn't even ask for my ID, they just waved us in. We had a great time! Beer's not my thing, but vodka doesn't taste like anything at all!

April 26th

Harry and I are making progress. Remember that shirt he got me last month? Well, this time, he bought me a leather skirt. It's soft red and soooo chic, it's to die for! It's short, but I'm all of a sudden at the forefront of fashion and it feels good.

With all the weight I've lost, he says that the skirt was made for me, that I'll look like a "slick hot chick". Harry says that the next thing on his list is a pair of shoes.

I asked him for a hat and he laughed and said: "Don't get your hopes up, I'm not that particular." I wonder what he meant.

May 15th

Harry and I are an "item", that's what Nic says. She doesn't like him much, and says that he's mean. I don't know where she got that idea! Harry's such a gentleman! Maybe a bit Gothic I suppose because he's almost always in black jeans, black silk shirt and black leather jacket. What can I say? It's just his color. The other girls are jealous of me and I'm proud that he chose me over them.

The weather is starting to warm up. Mom is getting some of her plants in and out of the house every night, except she lost two tomato plants yesterday. Must have a tomato plant robber somewhere in the neighborhood.

May 20th

Harry called. He's just lost his job at the weekend rich place. They hired someone else to drive their limo full-time. He's EMO right now, but I told him it was okay, that he'd find a better job soon and he still had wheels.

I asked him if he still had his job at the restaurant and he sort of stopped, then said: "Oh yeah, the restaurant. I'm thinking of changing jobs all together." When I asked him what he'd like to do, he said maybe security guard or something like that.

I told him it would probably help a lot in his career then asked him why he was taking machining at Tec Voc if he wanted to be a lawyer?

He laughed and replied that I was smarter than he'd realized. Machining was just something he'd always liked and figured it might come in handy if he ever got to represent common people in court. I suppose if I were ever to need a lawyer, having him tell me that he'd worked as a laborer might help me.

I wonder if Harry thought I was dumb. Or maybe he just didn't make the link between security, police and law? That can't be right. He's smart and he knows his stuff.

Ying Yang. What goes around comes around, like he says. Maybe he just wants me to be quiet and helpless. Maybe he likes me like that.

And maybe he's right: law and security guard don't have to be part of the same thing.

May 22nd

Tomorrow is Harry's birthday. I got him a really nice card. It's got a scale like those justice ones we see for the law courts and it says that the scales of justice have noticed that someone's up for a sentence. Inside it says that the sentence is 'to enjoy your Happy Birthday!

I hope he likes it.

May 23rd

What's gotten into him? He got so mad at me today, I got scared. And all over a birthday card!

When he opened the envelope, he got so pale I thought he was going to pass out! Then he looked up at me and grabbed my arm, so tight, I thought he was going to break it!

Then he said something really weird. "Who have you been talking to?"

I said nobody. Then I asked him to open the card. He did this with his other hand, and then he sort of let my arm go.

He said thanks then told me not to expect to see him for a few days. He said he needed some time to calm down.

Why does he need to calm down? Why did he accuse me of getting the card from somebody else? I asked him that and he turned on me and said to mind my own business.

I told him it was my business when he talked to me like that.

He grabbed me by the shoulders, kissed me hard, but didn't get a chance to go any further because Mrs. Bibeau came around the corner right then.

She didn't smile at either of us and asked Harry what he was doing in the hallway.

He kind of started stuttering and I looked at him in surprise because he's never done that before. Mrs. B raised her eyebrows and asked him why he wasn't in class? He backed up a step from me and fumbled for an answer. He really looked flustered, especially when our teacher just stood there, staring him down.

I saw Harry swallow hard before he bent down and whispered to meet him in the back after school that he had something to tell me. I nodded and he turned to head for class. When I turned back to Mrs. B, she shook her head and walked back the way she'd come. I wonder what she thought of finding us and will she report us to Mr. F, the school director?

I met Harry like he'd asked, but he was so weird! I showed him the bruises he gave me on my arms from this morning's episode and you know what he said? "You can always wear long shirts for a bit. But it won't happen again, I promise sweetheart. You're too precious to me, Teena."

Then he gave me a kiss and everything just felt right! It's so cool when we make up!

May 27th

Almost the end of the school year. Amazing! You'd think I could be all excited? Well, not really because Harry says that he won't be able to go out with me as much because he'll be leaving at the end of June to go work full-time in a summer camp on an island somewhere in Ontario.

June 8th

Tomorrow, Harry's asked me to wear something special, because he's taking me out to celebrate our relationship. Just to please him, I'm going to wear the shirt and skirt he bought me. I'm hoping he'll provide the shoes he's promised me.

June 9th

Harry canceled our date. He has to work, so I stayed home and Mom says I had on my sulking pout face. I don't care! This is the first time Harry hasn't come to pick me up! I miss him!

June 15th

Harry had to work overtime last week at his restaurant job because the other relief host was sick, so I've forgiven him. Harry asked me if I wanted to go to The Ex at the end of the month with him.

That's a kind of carnival with lots of rides, a Ferris wheel, a couple of roller coasters and this year is supposed to hold a show at the main stage - *Thousand Foot Crutch* is coming! They're awesome! I heard them last year at Mission Fest and they really have a strong message for youths. I bought one of their CD's and it's one of my favorites.

Nic says she's got tickets for the show. I'm hoping Harry has too.

I said, guess what? Yes! And Mom's said that as long as there is Nic, Cheryl and their boyfriends with us that we can go as a group. Yeah! Thunder Mountain, death defying rides! Watch out, because here I come!

June 25th

Mom's best friend Laura called her tonight. She's expecting her third baby and Mom's her birthing coach. Her husband Jim is with the military and is on a tour of duty in Afghanistan. She gave Mom a cell phone and said she'd call her on it when she went into labor.

June 26th

The Ex starts tonight, and Harry and I and the rest of the gang are going tomorrow night. I can't wait!

June 27th

I just got a delivery package and guess what was in it? The most beautiful pair of shoes! White, with slim heels and straps that make my feet look so elegant! And a pair of pantyhose, you know the kind that has squares, black lines, sort of like diamonds and sheer.

You know what else? The box was tied with a red rose and white ribbon. When I took the ribbon off, I saw that the rose was a wrist corsage! Plus it's the same color as my skirt! There's a note with it that asks me to wear the whole outfit that he gave me. I can't wait for tonight to come!

June 28th

I hate him! I hate him! I hate, hate, hate, *HATE* him! I can't believe I loved and that I let him rule me like that! How wrong I was. How stupid I was. I hurt so much!

Harry tricked me! Sure we went to the Ex, but Nic and Cheryl didn't even show up! Now I'm wondering if he ever invited them or if he lied about us meeting them.

Did I do something wrong? Maybe the clothes he gave me were on purpose? He had his arm around my waist because I kept losing my balance on those darn shoes! After only two hours of fun, we got in this black convertible he borrowed from a friend and we drove out of town a little bit.

The Ex's grounds aren't far from the perimeter, so he said he knew of this real special place where we could be by ourselves. Ooh! This is so hard to write! But I have to tell someone! Mom's not home! Laura is probably in labor!

I have to put this down on paper! I need to remember not to trust older, arrogant, smooth-talking men! There wasn't anybody around this special place he took me to! I started to feel a bit nervous, but he said it was still early, to just watch the stars come out. He put his arm around my shoulders and passed me his cigarette. When I said no, he pressed me to try just a puff, but I didn't feel like it, so he finished it, then sat back and gazed at the stars with me.

It's so weird writing about this as if it never happened to me, but I need to get this off my chest, need to talk to somebody about what happened. It's like the whole thing is crystal clear, like a carving behind my eyelids. And my ears! It's going to be even longer trying to erase what he told me.

I hate that! I wish I could just open a door in my brain, stuff what happened tonight in it and close the door and let it rot and dry out. But I can't. It hurts! Oh God! It hurts!

He started by kissing my cheek, then my earlobes and I didn't suspect a thing!

He then said that as we weren't too far from town, maybe we should head for a little park he knew of. I said why not go to a bar instead, but he said he didn't feel in the mood. He wanted to walk where we wouldn't hear the noise of car and truck traffic. A magical place he knew of.

I was so naive! So dumb! Couldn't I see where this was going? It's as if I was deaf and blind all of a sudden!

He headed out by Roblin Blvd and Assiniboine Park. We got out of the car and went for a walk and it was romantic. I didn't see it coming! Honest, I didn't!

Ooh! If only I didn't have to write about this, but, I need to tell somebody, and Mom might be at the hospital with her friend. She was due tonight! Oooh! It hurts so much!

2:30 a.m.

Harry, that scumbag! I hate him!!! I have to write about this. I really have to write this down. You're my only witness and hope Diary. I don't want anyone else to know!

He was kissing me so often, that I lost track of where we were exactly. When he finally lifted his head and hugged me to him, I realized we were in a clearing and there wasn't a path anywhere near!

"Harry," I breathed, "where are we?"

"Close now, my sweet Christina. Just be patient."

He had his hand under my shirt. I didn't suspect anything! His kissing kept getting deeper and deeper. When I tried to pull back from him, he grabbed my hair and kept on crushing his lips to mine.

I was scared and started to scream, but he slapped my cheek and told me to shut up! Then he dragged me deeper into the forest until there were just trees around us.

I remember being out of breath and trying to scream, him shoving me to the ground and pressing my face into the earth. I'll always remember the smell of wet, rotting leaves and the sound of his heavy breathing. He ran his hands up and down my legs and then very fast he ripped my pantyhose to shreds. Oh God! Please let me finish this! I don't want to remember anything else, but I know that I need to write it out! It's the only way to purge my head of the images!

I tried to move away from him, but he turned me back up and crushed his lips to mine. I tried to roll away but he grabbed my shoulders and literally pinned me down, then he ripped my shirt off, leaving me with only the light blue camisole I wore under it. He pushed that up under my armpits and started biting at my breasts. When I shied away, he grabbed my hair and pushed my head back down with kisses that were overpowering. They were dangerous. They made me feel afraid. So afraid! I prayed to God that he wouldn't kill me or that he wouldn't cut me up in little pieces!

"Get off of me! Please Harry! You're scaring me! Please! Get off of me!" I kept telling him to get off, but he wouldn't. He wouldn't!!!

He laughed! "You're the one that's been goading me beyond endurance, dressing like a slut! Look at the shirt you're wearing. It's the trap you've wanted me to fall in all this time. You're out of options, sweet Chris. Trust me now. It's time you faced the music."

He slapped my face when I tried to claw him away from me and the next second he laughed and said: "I like feistiness. Now calm down before I get mad. "

How could I ever have trusted him? He rolled me over some rocks, then grabbed my arms and kissed me again. Then he used his knee to keep me down.

I tried to fight him, but then he grabbed my skirt and pushed it up and...... oooh! It hurts so much!

His hand just invaded my private parts. I thought he just wanted to get closer, but then he... lowered my panties and....I tried to fight back by crossing my legs, but he slapped my face again and told me to behave and lie quiet or else. He sounded angry, but I fought all the same!

"Harry! Stop! Please stop! You're hurting me!"

"I love it when you all fight back." He laughed long and hard. "That makes the journey much more adventurous."

I tried so hard to stop him! But he unhooked my legs and.... sat on my thighs... undid his jeans….

"Noooo! Stop! Harry! Please stop right now! I'll do anything you want me to do, just don't-"

I heard a scream and realized it was me! Then he punched me in the mouth. And invaded me again, and again, and again. And hit me, again and again!

I don't remember anything after that, because I think I passed out. When I came to, he was still there. Standing over me, laughing at me as he got dressed.

I tried to get up, but couldn't move! I felt paralyzed and so sick! He laughed at my attempts to get up. Just as I thought he was going to leave me, he knelt over me and leered. Then he …. ooh! I can't say it! He covered my mouth with his hand and took a knife out of his pocket, opened it and held it to my throat!

"If you dare say anything to anybody, I'll come back and haunt your days, got it? You've had this coming to you, you slut!" He spit in my face and went on. "Next time I won't be so gentle. You'll not see the light of day ever again." He pressed the blade against my windpipe. "Promise or I kill you here and now."

I remember swallowing really nervously and I didn't want to agree with him, but he pushed again with the knife and I felt something hot and burning. That's when I decided that he wasn't playing games and if I didn't agree, he was going to kill me. I nodded and he straightened, stood before kicking me over some rocks like I was a bag of potatoes and left me to die.

4 a.m.

I don't know how long it was before I even dared to move. I could hear him walking back and forth and I didn't want him to come back and hurt me again. I don't know how long I stayed huddled against the pain and burning. All I know is that I waited a long time before moving, breathing or even crying. I was hoping he would go away and leave me alone and maybe think I was dead, because I don't ever want to see him again! I could hear his laughter even as he moved away from me and then he came back and dropped my shirt over me! I didn't dare move! I kept thinking that if he thought I was unconscious or dead that he'd leave me and go away.

I don't know how long I waited there, barely breathing, waiting and waiting and waiting to be sure he was gone. All I know is that sometime later, when I cautiously opened my eyes, I couldn't hear anything except the buzz of mosquitoes around me. I sat up and tried to stand but I fell over. My shirt fell off and I tried to put it on, but it was ripped so bad that I decided I might as well leave it there.

I kept my camisole on; at least I wouldn't be indecent.

I crawled forward, wanting to be anywhere but where I was. I found my purse a few feet away and the money Mom always says is to be used for emergencies. I finally was able to grab the trunk of a tree and pull myself up.

I walked a long time before finding a path that looked like it went somewhere. I remember thanking God for a clear sky and a full moon. And for guiding my steps to a sidewalk and civilization.

I know I was crying. I think God made sure there was a pay phone booth at a closed gas station because I don't remember it ever being there before. Or maybe I walked further than I think.

I called a cab and then sank down on the bench next to the phone. My hands were shaking a lot, but I straightened my clothes as best I could in the light from the booth. Those were the longest minutes in my life! All I wanted was to go home.

The cab driver was an old man and he had to help me stand, I was so shaky.

He wanted to take me straight to the hospital, but I said no. I didn't need that. I wanted my bed, my house and my mom.

I said I lived across from the cops, so if it was the same to him, I just wanted to go home. Home where it's safe to be. Safe from HIM!

5 a.m.

I read that entry now, and I can still feel the fear rising up in me. That irrational fear that makes you realize that you have no control over the situation, that there's only you and nobody else around, that even if you scream, no one will hear you or come to your rescue. And then I realize that I trusted my virginity and body to the scum of the earth.

I feel so helpless. So scared! What if he comes here? What if he tries to break down the door? What if he's watching me even now? Oh God! Help!

I'm so shaky, I can hardly hold my pen. My stomach's not doing the greatest either!

June 29th

I'm scared to tell Mom. Oh God! The phone is ringing! What if it's him? What if-- No, it's Mom. She's leaving a message on the answering machine. Laura's gone into labor! I guess I'll see her when she comes home.

She says there's no rush to come home. If I want to stay over at Nic's for another night it's okay with her.

8 a.m.

The phone is ringing again! What if he breaks down the front door?

I wish Nic was here. Maybe she'd be able to hold me together. Maybe if I went to her place?

I can't! I can't! Every time I move it hurts so much! All I can do is write about it in here. I am going nuts! I'm so scared!

June 30th

Mom is still with Laura. I heard her voice on the answering machine say that there are complications with the birth. Nic called too, but I can't seem to move off the bed. And I can't close my eyes either!

Every time I do, I feel him pushing me down, his cruel hands almost breaking my bones! The terror of the night filling me up again and again!

I found some bruises on my arms and legs, but I'm too afraid to take off my clothes. What if - Oh, God! Why did this have to happen to me? What did I do wrong?

Was it my clothes? The way I acted? Was it because I didn't smoke Harry's cigarette?

I have to try to take off my clothes. Maybe a bath is going to help wash him off me.

I can't!!!! I can't move! *Oh, God! Please help me out with this! I don't want to feel like this for the rest of my life! Please send Mom home!*

Every time I try to take off my clothes, my hands freeze and I can't even undo a single thing. Can't even take off the stupid shoes or the skirt! And I can't stop shaking!

July 2nd

It was Canada's birthday yesterday. I asked Mom to bring me my diary, because I need to unload on someone else than her. The night of the.... oh, when will I be able to say that word? Harry did this to me!

Two adults from the police department's Victim's Bureau came to see me yesterday after the doctor examined me. They asked if I wanted to press charges against the person who did this to me. The doctor asked me that when he first saw me in Emergency, but I guess I was in shock, because I couldn't stop shaking and I couldn't make up my mind.

Mom found me crying on my bed last night. She took one look at me and pulled me into her arms. Then she wrapped me in a blanket, I was so cold! She and I cried together and then she took me to the hospital.

I'll never, as long as I live, forget that wild ride! I think Mom broke every rule of the road!

The doctor touched in some really sore spots, but he was able to document that I was r... attacked sexually and that all we can do now is wait and see.

He wanted me to take a pill so that I have less chances of getting pregnant, but I said that I didn't want to. My body belongs to God and I'm positive I'm not at a time in my cycle where I could get pregnant.

5:30 p.m.

The police came to see me again this afternoon; this time two officers like Mom's renters. They asked me all kinds of questions and mostly wanted to know where HE did this to me. It's a bit hazy.... like I'm not sure anymore. I know we went to a forest, but I'm not sure where.

July 3rd

When Mom drove me to the hospital, she kept telling me that I needed to press charges against Harry, but I was too confused then to agree or not. HIS last words were still ringing in my ears.

"If I hear that you spread lies about me, I'll personally hunt you down and make sure that you won't have anything else to say for eternity."

After the face-to-face talk Mom and I had last night, I'm going ahead with the charges.

See, Mom was attacked sexually when she was twenty two. *That's* how she got pregnant with me and that's one of the reasons she left home. Her parents disowned her, telling her that what she had done was a shameful act! It wasn't her fault! We have a lot more in common than what I ever thought. She says she chose not to press charges against the man who did that to her because she was scared he'd come after her. My father went on to attack six other girls from her hometown and murdered the last one. Under the circumstances I'm glad she waited to tell me who he really was. I asked a lot of questions when I found out she came from Riverton. No wonder she didn't want to tell me about the man who is the tenth of my person.

Maybe HE's done the same too. I'm hoping, like Mom says, that by bringing Harry to justice, that no one else will have to suffer. The creep!

I think I understand why he reacted so strongly to the birthday card I gave him. If he's done that before and the cops were after him, no wonder he reacted the way he did. I wonder if he really intended to go to law school. Maybe that was a lie. Maybe on purpose.

July 10th

Harry's in for a surprise. After talking with the Victim's Bureau again, the case worker said that it takes guts to charge a person who's committed an attack like what HE did to me. It's considered to be a violent act of assault and it will receive the same sentencing as a homicide, especially since he threatened me with a knife.

The case worker is a woman and she gave me some statistics. She says that sexual assault is an "expression of violence, not sexual desire." She also said that it usually is done as a 'date rape' and that it is almost always premeditated and executed. That very often these incidences are executed in the same way as a murder, that every little detail is planned! She also said that sometimes, the assaults follow a pattern and that helps the cops pinpoint assaults to a particular person. Talk about CSI!!!!!

Her name's Marcia. She's so tiny you'd think that she'd have had to ask the cops to lift her into the squad cars, but she's full of spunk, like Mom says.

Marcia says that sexual assault is the most profound invasion of a person's body and that Harry will be charged to the full extent of the law. Would you believe that she congratulated me for charging HIM? I'm still scared to have him come to our house but I feel better about my decision to charge him because, like Mom says: 'It will help you face your fears head on instead of isolating you in terror.'

July 12th

They found and arrested Harry today. I'm not sure how I feel. Relieved? Sure, to a certain extent.

I guess angry is probably the closest. He tricked me and I fell for it! I should have seen the signs.

Remember when he got angry at the word "opaque"? And the Birthday card? I should have walked away from him then. Walked away and not have had anything more to do with him.

But Mom says that hindsight is always 20/20 and that you can't change the past, only the future.

So how am I supposed to stop this anger and fear and guilt and tears?

July 15th

It's been a roller coaster of emotions. I'm so confused; I don't know where to turn! I'm out of the hospital, but I'm having trouble sleeping. Every time I fall into a deep sleep, I see HIM coming after me! I feel his hands on me and I remember the pain. I remember the feeling of panic and helplessness when he held that knife to my throat.

Mom says to give myself time. She said that she'd gone through the same process herself. It helps, but I wish I could feel better quickly.

I saw Marcia again. Harry's been warned not to have any contact with me. Apparently he's done this type of "thing" before. (Remember that pattern thing?) Maybe he thought that I was gullible enough that I wouldn't tell anyone, although he once called me 'smart'.

My laying charges was the droplet that made the coffee overflow. He's wanted in Saskatchewan and Ontario on twelve - can you believe it? Twelve counts of assault and sexual assault! It makes me wonder how he was even able to attend CLR? Did he really fail those grades or did he simply forge documents so that he could infiltrate our school?

The cops said that I was lucky. Out of the twelve, not including me, eight of them have been maimed for life. Seems they fought when he took the knife to their throats. I remember praying

God to save me from any serious wounds that night. God came through for me.

Ugh! Thank God HE's out of my life. Mom says that the police almost posted his bail, but they rescinded that decision when they found out that he's wanted for questioning in two other provinces. He's under lock and key for now. Now I have to wait for a trial date. Marcia also told me that if he had been let go 'on bail', that they'd have issued him an ankle bracelet that would track his movements. Sort of like a GPS. Good thing. He's a wily eel! Marcia says he's got a pattern of pleading not guilty and pulling up a lawyer out of thin air who has pulled him out of prison more times than not.

Maybe Harry is a billionaire? On a - oops, gross! Talk about me trying to find excuses! Why do I fall for these guys? Why do I weaken like that? Won't I ever have a normal dating life? Get a boyfriend that treats me with love and respect?

Mom keeps telling me that I've got Jesus, but I want someone to hold me in his arms, tell me he loves me for me, not because I'm skinny or thin or a sex object!

I mean, me, Teena Danais? Oh God! What's wrong with me? Will I ever be okay? *Ever?*

The cops that park in those two spots out back each gave me a shoulder squeeze last time they saw me. I suppose they know. I'm not too comfortable around men right now. And isn't it weird that it's a different feeling of fear than when I was "arrested" with Charlie? Speaking of her, it makes me wonder about Harry.

Both he and Charlie were liars. Does that mean that I can't and won't ever be able to make the right kind of friends?

I was just as gullible with Charlie as I was with Harry. Both of them were cheaters and liars! Oh, God! I wish I'd never met either one!

July 30th

Mom introduced me to Mrs. Dora this afternoon. She has no dress sense. She's got gray hair, pretty straggly and wears these huge glasses that keep sliding down her nose. Her voice is cool though. Really cool. I mean, not cold, but..... hmmmm, hard to describe. She made me see some things I never would have thought to look for in a guy and also some things about me I didn't even know. Like the fact that I'm a strong person and that I can and will recover from this. That I did everything that I could and not to feel guilty about not doing what I think was the best.

She said that "no matter what we do, some people will always be stronger than us, that when a perp (short for perpetrator, which is the person who attacks or is the criminal) wants something and he's goaded beyond his already volatile (over the edge anger) emotions, that it would take three men to control him". She said I was "lucky that he left you before he killed you". That started me crying and shaking.

She's so right, that sometimes I'm amazed! I survived the rape! Hey! I can say it and write it now! I guess Mrs. Dora would be proud. She said that until I could say it, the incident would always stay an "accident" in my mind and not an actual happening, an invasion of my privacy.

You know, she's right. I know I was raped by Harry and that what he did to me was wrong.

Mrs. Dora says that one out of every two women will become a victim of sexual assault at some point in her lifetime. That is too scary for thought!

August 1st

Mom has been helping me too. She didn't tell me what had happened to her when she was raped, because she said that each rape is different and that talking about it, only brought the nightmares back for her.

But she said the important thing to remember was that, although she got pregnant, I came into her life at a time when she knew she was ready to have and raise a child on her own if need be. She reminded me that although the man was my father, that there was no way that I had inherited his killing genes and not to worry about it.

Mrs. Dora said that that was an important thing to remember too. And If I do get pregnant, it's important to remember that it is the parent who raises the child that will have the most impact on that child's life, not the man who started the whole process.

August 4th

I had another interview with Marcia. She said that it was important that I visit the site where the rape occurred. I really don't want to do that, but she said I needed to see that it was no longer an area that I need to be afraid of.

She also said that for some teens, the location of a sexual assault often traumatizes them and that they have a tendency to stay away from some such areas for the rest of their lives unless they deal with it while it is still fresh in their minds.

Mom's coming with me and I hope that.... everything goes..... well enough so that I won't feel traumatized for the rest of my life!

10 p.m.

It was amazing! Marcia was right! I feel a lot better.

You can't tell! She said that when they were first there, that they did find some stuff they can use in the trial and certainly that awful shirt and shred of pantyhose, so that's a plus and she did say that my memory will eventually recover and that I'll be able to use the anger against Harry to keep me going during the trial.

Sigh. Trial..... I'll have to testify against him. I don't want to! I'm scared! What if he comes to get me later on in my life?

What then? Am I doing the right thing in prosecuting him?

August 8th

Dora and I are pretty good friends. I'm finding out that I can make better decisions for myself. I'm glad to a certain extent that I'm still on holidays and that none of my friends, like Nic and Cheryl are around this summer. At least the bruises are all gone. Now if my heart could just melt a little of that fear that Harry will show up at the door or call me.

I know he's in prison, but he could escape and come for me first!

August 15th

It's been one and a half months since the rape and I still haven't had my period. I'm getting worried. What if....?

August 16th

I went to the library today to check my e-mail messages then I thought I'd play a game. You know what I typed in the search window? *Adbroption!* Would you believe the computer actually asked me if I meant abortion or adoption? It also tells me what's on my mind, that thing that's not going away. The stress that's keeping me awake at night! The pain and fear of finding out if I'm.... NO! I'M NOT EVEN GOING TO THINK ABOUT IT!!!

August 18th

Still nothing. I'm scared.

August 20th

I threw up even before breakfast this morning. I think I'm going to have to go to a pharmacy for one of those kits. I don't really want to, but.... what if...... ?

August 24th

It's still in the box. I take it out and look at it, but I don't want to find out. I'm just too afraid to try.

August 25th

Mom found the box on my bed. I was looking at it when I got up this morning, and she caught me puking in the bathroom. She had a sad smile on her face when I came up for air. Then she said: "Let's do this together, okay? That way, you'll know for sure, and we'll at least know where to start." I asked her to wait one more day. But she said the longer I waited, the harder it would be to do it. So I gave in.

It's positive. I'm pregnant. PREGNANT!

PART TWO

Doing The Right Thing – "I will deliver
you from all oppression."

Luke 4:18

August 26th

Pregnant with a baby I know I'm not going to be able to take care of. What am I going to do? Mom just held me in her arms after the test and then she had to go to work. She wanted to stay with me, but with the trial looming, she's going to need every penny of the three jobs.

I'm still not finished crying. I'm bawling now.

August 27th

Mom and I are at the Crisis Pregnancy Center. I'm in distress all right. How can people laugh here? Don't they know when we first come here that we hurt, that we're miserable?

Mom's just put her arm around my shoulder. She says to remember that it's okay to laugh when you're happy. That quite soon, I'll be laughing too.

How can she say that? I'm the victim here! I have a right to be angry, to be moody, and to be in tears! Mom says to look on the other side of the coin. It could mean that they have a positive outlook on life.

Maybe I can live with this. Mrs. Dora says I'm stronger than I think.

Maybe I can be positive, live through this blunder, this pain and this horrible horror.

I feel like I've been transported into a horror movie where the heroine is crushed and bruised by the great escape out of the chamber of torture.

If only I could blink my eyes and everything would go back to how it was before.

If only I didn't have this bunch of cells growing in me, wanting to rule my life!

What if my friends leave me? What if I even lose Nic's friendship?

Woah! That's enough to give me nightmares! She's working at a summer camp outside the city this year and I can't just call her up and tell her this over the phone. *Oh God!* I'm crying for the silliest of things.

Mom says it's normal, but, maybe there's something really wrong with me? I just can't stop crying!

It's so weird! I mean, there's this creature growing in me and I know I'm not ready to have a kid! I'm only seventeen and a half!!!! I want to be more than what Mom has been.

She had dreams of medical school and what happens? She gets me and hasn't been able to go. She works in hotels and waitresses in pubs and bartends for weddings! What kind of a life is that?

God, why were you so cruel to her? She didn't do anything wrong! Mom is - well - I wonder if she ever thought of abortion. How come she didn't go that route? How come... oh, I guess I should ask her that when she comes out of the washroom instead of you.

And that brings up another point. Do I want this baby to know that his - biological sperm donor - raped me?

I want to be something more than what Mom got to be. I have to make a decision here. I have to decide what I'm going to do. Abortion, adoption or keep it? My head hurts just thinking about keeping it. Remember Monster? Like I could really be a good mother? Christina Danais. A baby in her belly. A child to hold.

I just can't picture myself with a baby in my arms! Take that abortion pill and ask God for forgiveness? But that's wrong! I don't want to kill. God says not to kill.

So then adoption? Are there alternatives? But, I wouldn't know who this baby would get for parents. He deserves better than what I can give him, better than what I got. He deserves two parents that will raise him up to be a responsible Canadian citizen. He deserves the love of two parents, a mother AND a father!

8 p.m.

We're home! Well, I've got another counselor. Sherry. She's really nice. She's older, but not as much as Mrs. Dora and she dresses real nice. She held my hands when I started crying and told me it's perfectly normal to feel weepy. Apparently being pregnant does that to you. Your hormones are all twisted. She says that I'll also start to want to go to the bathroom to pee a lot more than before.

Oh, joy! Who needs this? Sherry says that it's normal to feel upset and scared and confused. Being pregnant is not easy and she and I had a frank talk about what I see this baby doing later.

She also encouraged me to talk about the assault. It helped a lot to unload that part of my life.

She said I had every right to be upset and angry. What Harry did to me is a crime and he needs to be punished for it, but she also reminded me that God will punish Harry in His own way and that if I put my trust in God, that all will fall into place.

I told her about praying while Harry held the knife to my throat, about keeping me from wounds and she said it was very courageous of me to have done that and that God is always present in that type of situation. That even though we might think that He has abandoned us, He hasn't. That His hand is ALWAYS upon us. No matter where we are, no matter what we're doing or how. It's a comforting thought.

We talked about the different options open to me. Abortion is not the answer for me, neither is keeping the baby. So, she gave me some packages of papers to read. One of them is a leaflet about adoption procedures.

Do you know that in my city, there are only four options for adoption? A private adoption agency, Family and Child Protection Services (FCPS) - they take babies and children that have no parents or whose parents don't want them or that aren't nice to them and place them in foster homes.

I've always wondered where those kids came from.... I always thought that the kids were from abusive families or abandoned or from druggies, but Sherry says that FCPS takes and places children up to the ages of sixteen in foster homes when the situation in which they are in is dangerous to their mental, physical or emotional stability. They are also an alternative to a private adoption agency. They place babies in adoption to parents that really want them!

I'm certain that this is not an agency for me. I don't want this baby to be put up for adoption in a system that has mostly foster parenting. Maybe this child would end up going from home to home. No stability. Plus, how will I know if the parents he gets are good parents?

And then there's a family member. Mom said that when she got pregnant with me, she moved to the city where her own family wouldn't interfere with her raising of me. She said that she could have put me up for adoption with her parents, but they weren't the best of parents in the first place and she didn't want that for me.

Sherry says that if I choose that option, that the parents-to-be are screened and visited before any child is put with them. This is done by FCPS and through a lawyer.

She said that a lawyer is important because he does all the legal paperwork and makes sure that everything is according to the Manitoba Adoption Act and Regulations. If I decide to go that route, I have to sign a "*Voluntary placement agreement with a child and family services agency to permit time for the birth parent to make an informed decision regarding adoption placement of the child;*"

I'm quoting that from the adoption act because I'm stuck on the mumbo jumbo. I guess that means I have to sign over all rights of ever seeing this baby after he's adopted.

There's also another thing in here. It says that sometimes adoption agencies look to place the baby in the same culture as the birth parent. I wouldn't mind that!

August 28th

Today was my first appointment with my own doctor. He says I'm in good health and that if everything goes well, I can expect a beautiful and healthy baby sometime in April next year. But I DON'T WANT A BABY!!!!! He's sending me to an obstetrician. That's a doctor that delivers just babies. BABIES!!!! Rabies!

August 30th

I DON'T WANT THIS KID! I don't want to feel stuck like a duck in our house or laughed at in school this fall. I don't want to be pitied either! Why, God? Why did I let this happen to me? Couldn't I have seen this coming? Why was I so stupid? Stupid! Stupid!

September 4th

First day of school. I don't want to be here. I want to be someplace else, where I don't know anybody, where they don't remind me of Harry.

Nic and Veronique asked me where he was. I just said that he and I broke up and that I didn't want to talk about it. It's over.

Ugh! I'm glad he's out of my life! His trial comes up in December. The judge at his bail trial said that he was to have no contact with me, but he's tried. I still cringe. Remember that night? I was so afraid he'd come?

Mom had to hire a lawyer through the legal system so we could get a Restraining Order against him. That way, if he calls or shows up here, we have something to show the cops and they can come and take him away.

I don't ever, EVER, EVER, want to see him! But Sherry says that it's important that I do face him that it will help me heal inside. I'm not so sure about that.

September 15th

I met the baby doctor today. He's an obstetrician. He's a lot younger than I thought he'd be. More around Mom's age. And he isn't as stuffy as our family doctor.

Dr. Ross says that everything is going well. He asked me if I want to keep my baby. But I told him that it's not my baby. It's Harry's and I don't intend on raising it myself.

He looked a bit surprised, but then he asked if I had thought of abortion. I did, but somehow, God, (who is back in my life) is telling me something different.

I'm not ready to raise a child on my own. Even if Mom helped me out, this baby would be too difficult to raise.

Remember Monster? Nic and Mom could handle him but I only made him cry! Plus, it costs a lot of money to raise a kid. I can just imagine how much!

In the Baby-Think-It-Over program, we were given fake money to buy what the doll needed. Diapers and formula is expensive! I checked it out at the store the other day when we went shopping. Just a pair of socks, a "sleeper" (that's what a baby wears for a few months as clothes) is over 20 dollars!

And a baby dirties his clothes a lot more than I do! Can you just imagine Mom and I trying to keep up with everything money-wise and a baby on top? She'll need to go out and work a fourth job and I'll have to work too! And on only half-hour naps? I'll be dead before I graduate!

Plus, Mom would remember too much of the sacrifices that she's already doing for me and she'd never get anywhere but end up deeper in debt than what we are now.

No. No abortion and no keeping it either. Adoption is the only thing that will work.

September 22nd

Dora and I are good friends now. She's made me look at Harry with reality check eyes. That's hard to swallow, even now. Harry was a "take advantage of the situation" kind of guy. He manipulated you to do things against your will, and made you think you'd agreed to do them, or made you think you had thought them up yourself.

He was this guy from the Dark Ages. Cave man stuff. Pull your hair and slap you around a lot and then turn around and say: "Well, you asked for it."

No, I didn't ask for it, and you certainly won't ask for anything else. You and I are done, finished, finito, kaputski!

October 9th

Mom and I started looking at our options. She said that we need to have an idea of what to ask the agencies, like FCPS and the adoption agency so that we can compare notes and come up with the best decision based on knowledge rather than on point and pin the tail on the donkey.

October 13th

I'm finding it really difficult to be in school. I'm starting to "show" like Sherry says and some of my friends are starting to ask weird questions. They think I'm gaining weight again. I'm too scared to tell them the real reason for the little bulge. I talked it over with Sherry and she gave me this pamphlet on the Teen Parent Center. Maybe that's my next step.

59

October 15th

Mom and I have an appointment with the director of the Teen Center. We're going to decide together if this is the way to go or if it would be better if I was tutored at home. I hope I don't have to go to the center. I can't explain it. It just feels wrong. I've been praying about it, and it doesn't feel right.

As if I was turning my back on my own school. But, can I face everyone at school? What are they going to say? Will they laugh at me? Will Jerry-The-Bully beat me up? Will he call me worse than 'Dough Girl'? Will Nic still want to be my friend?

October 17th

Well, we went.... and as soon as we stepped in, I got this horrible feeling! It just wouldn't go away!

It wasn't like the lady wasn't nice or anything, but seeing all those girls pregnant and the classes of parenting that I'd be taking scared me half to death!

I'm not going to be the parent! I'm going to make sure that this baby is well taken care of, that the parents he gets are the best for him!

When we were in the car Mom just asked: "So?"

I hadn't the heart to tell her that I didn't want to go there. So I didn't answer her.

She stopped the car on the side of the road and took me in her arms and hugged me. She said:

"Teena honey, you don't have to decide right away. We've got other options to look at."

I cried all over her. It's weird. Sherry did say that I would cry a lot, but I didn't think it would be this much!

October 19th

I've reached a decision. I'm going to stay at CLR Collegiate. My friends are all there, they know me and I'm growing. I'm graduating this year. I want to be part of the class! So what if I'm pregnant? So what if I have a bulging stomach? So? They can take me like I am or not at all!

Sherry said that fear can paralyze a person, but fear can also be used wisely when you channel it towards a positive outcome.

If there's one thing I've learnt from Charlie and Harry, it's that I now refuse to be a doormat. I am someone who, with the help of both Sherry and Mrs. Dora, is learning that I can hold my own counsel. I can make decisions on my own. And with God and Mom, those decisions will be the best ones for me and this baby.

October 23rd

Saw Dr. Ross again for a checkup and this time Mom couldn't come. She said she had to work extra hours if we're going to make it financially this month.

I never realized how tight her budget is! We don't often go out, but you know what sucks the most money? Her car! Lately it's been at the garage a lot.

Mom says it's the 'luck of the draw'. She says she figures she got a lemon.

What do sour fruits have to do with cars?

Dr. Ross says I should start to feel better, that my "morning sickness" should start to fade away soon. He showed me how big the fetus should be by now: about the size of my thumb. Thing he doesn't seem to understand is that this "thing" isn't MY baby. It's going to be someone else's responsibility!

October 26th

This week has been tough! Nic was speechless when I told her. Her mouth just dropped and she stared at me for the longest time! I had to laugh! It felt good to laugh.... I haven't done that too much.

Then, she hugged me tight and said she was sorry for what Harry did to me.

That was the best thing she could have told me. You know what I said to her?

"Charlie tried to get me arrested. Harry took advantage and manipulated me. Telling the rest of the graduating class can't be as bad."

Nic and I laughed so hard, this kid started moving! It felt like a tickle! Wow!

October 29th

Today's the day. I'm wearing the first of my maternity outfits that Mom found for me at the V V Boutique. I'm still in style, I mean, we all wear oversized shirts now, but I think class is going to be a bit difficult in first period.

I talked with Mrs. Bibeau day before yesterday and asked if it was all right to do my presentation on something that had to do with the subject we're studying this semester: discovering and finding yourself.

We're taking a book and it's pretty intense sexually and talks about just that. She went over the presentation structure with me and I bet she's going to be surprised out of her seat!

9 p.m.

Well, it wasn't quite what I expected! I didn't take my coat off until Mrs. B called me up to the front. I had six minutes to talk. That's awfully long when you don't know what to say, but with the plan that Mrs. B gave us, it was a lot easier than what I thought it would be.

I got up there and faced them all. Doug was in the front row and like usual, he snickered at me. Phil closed his eyes, crossed his arms and looked bored. Margaret started twirling her curls. (Thank God Jerry-The-Bully is not in my English Lit class!)

I looked over at Nic and she just smiled and showed me to take a deep breath. I said I had something important to share with the graduating class of this year and that it wasn't something that was going to be easy to talk about.

I also said that it was about being myself, about doing what was right and about choosing what was right for me.

Then I took off my coat and flattened my shirt against my stomach.

I heard gasps all over class and I prayed to God to help me say the right words. Now I believe what Mom's been telling me. He *does* help you when you're desperate! I told the class that sometime in April I would be missing classes because I would probably be delivering a baby.

I asked my class to just remember that I was still Teena, that I was still the same person they had grown up with, that this didn't change anything about me or my future.

That I had some tough decisions to make and that I wasn't keeping my baby but going to have him adopted into a family that could give him everything that he would need, because I wasn't ready to raise him like he ought to be raised.

I said that like the book says, being sexually active did carry a hefty penalty before marriage. It often got you in more trouble than what you bargained for. That to be a responsible human being, it meant that you had to keep your head screwed on straight, to think about others and to remember that life is too short to ruin someone else's life just because you got a high out of a moment in time.

Mrs. B had tears rolling down her cheeks at that point and I added just one more thing.

I said that I didn't want any of them to have pity on me, to continue to treat me like a human being, that although I was pregnant, it hadn't been consensual and that it was a crime.

Then I finished my presentation by saying a quote from Sherry.

"Rape is a sexual offense. It's an invasion of someone's privacy. It is a time where a man *or* woman has control over another's body. Your body belongs to God, because He created us and He's had his hand on us from the time we are conceived."

Then I went to sit at my desk.

I think you could have heard a pin drop in that room. When I looked up at the clock, I saw that I'd been up there for ten minutes and I hadn't even realized it! When I looked back at Nic, her eyes were full of tears and when I looked at the other guys around me, there was like this sense that it was something they hadn't ever heard or maybe it was just that no one has ever told them that there are consequences in life.

When I started putting my stuff away, I heard someone clap their hands, then two others joined in and before I knew it, the whole class was on their feet and clapping.

I tell you, I was speechless! I didn't know what to do! I just sat there looking at them all and wondering what to do next.

Mrs. B came up to me and put out a hand. I shook it. When I peeped at her, her eyes were wet and I read sadness and hurt in them. I wonder why?

November 2nd

You remember when I did my presentation in English Lit? Well, would you know it.... Mrs. B sent me a card at home! In it she says that she'd like to see me in eight days time during the lunch hour. She says she's got something to talk over with me. I wonder if it has anything to do with her reaction to my speech?

November 3rd

I'm not only showing, but this kid is kicking up a storm! I'm having trouble turning over in bed. There's like this space between my abdomen and the bed and it hurts when I lie on my side. I talked it over with Dr. Ross and he suggested I put a small cushion under it, that it should help relieve the muscle strain. He said it was normal.

I went to see Sherry today and she and I talked about adopting again. I don't feel comfortable with FCP and I know adopting for Mom is out of the question.

I know she's got relatives in Riverton, but in all these years she hasn't had much contact with them, so, getting this kid adopted by them isn't an option either.

So that left us with the private adoption agency. Mom and I poured over each one this past weekend and finally chose what we thinks is the best. Sherry says I won't have to pay anything to the agency, and she'll set up an appointment with them. I asked her to come with us because she's my friend and I know she knows more about all of this than Mom and I.

November 6th

Would you believe it? I'm wearing maternity pants! There's this stretchy sort of t-shirt fabric in the front of the pants and it gives my abdomen a place to grow. Sort of like the kangaroo pouch. And you know what the weirdest thing is? When I get up in the morning, I'm fairly comfortable, but when I'm ready for bed, it's like I've gained ten pounds! Really weird. And I have to go pee! A lot!!!!!

November 10th

Wow! I wouldn't have thought of anything like this ever happening! Mrs. B and Mrs. Chartier and Miss Crock were there. I thought it was just going to be Mrs. B but she said that she wanted the other two to hear what I had told the class. I said it would be difficult for me to tell it like I had said it then because I didn't have my notes with me.

Miss Crock said that what I was going through was probably really difficult for me right now and was there anything the counseling department could do to help me out? That floored me. I know they do stuff like that, like tutoring and getting social workers involved with some students, but, I've got good counseling already and I told them who I was seeing.

Then Mrs. Chartier said that if there was anything the Resource Center could do to help me through the month that I was supposed to deliver, that they would guide me through whatever it took to get me to Grad. I just stared at her!

That was more than I thought could happen.

I know that I'll have to take some time off to deliver this baby, but I thought that I could just come back to school the next day and keep on from there. The three teachers looked at each other and then smiled back at me.

Mrs. Chartier said I would probably miss about two months at least. And that's going to bring me to the end of May or beginning June! Are there ever a lot of details to deal with!

I'm glad I'm choosing adoption. I can't imagine having a baby at school until grad!

November 15th

First ultrasound. Dr. Ross just wanted me to have one to be sure that everything is going well. He says that I'm in good health, but that I'm gaining weight too fast and he wants to know why.

Do you know that I had to take time off school? And I had to drink this huge liter of water just before the test? I couldn't pee either. You know how hard that is?

I thought the first time the lady took that cold gel and put it on the sort of mike thing they use to 'see', that I was going to explode!

Then, she took the "wand" as she called it and glided it over to the side of my abdomen, then whoosh, back up to the middle, then over to the other side. She kept stopping it and keying in different numbers with the other hand on a computer screen.

I don't know what it will show, but I do know that I hope I never have another ultrasound. I'll never stop peeing!

Mom said that when she was pregnant with me, that they didn't have ultrasounds. I used to think that she didn't care about me, but she's really someone strong. It took guts to keep me, not only when she found out she was pregnant, but to move out of her hometown and come and live in the city. Whatever happened between her and her family must have been really bad if she hasn't been in contact with them all my life.

November 18th

First appointment at the adoption agency. There sure are a lot of papers and forms to fill in. I've got this big file of stuff to fill out before my next appointment and I'm supposed to get an adoption counselor.

Another one!

There's like .... Mrs. Dora, Sherry, Miss Crock at school.... and now more????

What else is there to talk about ?

If I have to talk to everyone of them in the same day I'll be as flat as the coyote in the Road Runner!

November 19th

You know, there was this long list of requirements that I had to fill out at the adoption agency on our second meeting. Things like what profession did I want to have for the parents, how much schooling they got, how many children in their family already, color of the hair and a whole bunch of other things!

It was so long, I had to ask the secretary if I could take the thing home. She said it was a good idea to discuss it with Mom too because she could help me through with what she'd gone through.

It was really cool, because Mom helped me figure out that if the adopting couple are out of the city, there wouldn't be much chance of me visiting after...... now I wonder if that's such a good idea? I'll have to ask.

And the secretary said that I have to prioritize what I put on that list.

What kind of Christian parents do I want this baby to have? How far away is rural for me? If they have pets, is it okay if they also live on a farm and have cows or pigs? And how old do I want the parents to be? That's a toughie.

There's that twenty one day clause too.... I'm still confused on that one.

November 20th

I'm seeing Dr. Ross today. His office called me to come for a special appointment. I wonder what's wrong? Could the baby be... dead?

4:30 p.m.

I think I'm in shock. I'm going to have twins! T-W-I-N-S!!!!

November 21st

I called Sherry and she got me in today. We had a long talk and she said that it probably won't matter with the adoption agency, but that it might make a placement more challenging.

She reminded me to keep praying for the family that will be receiving the baby – I mean babies! I'm doing that every morning and night now. I think it helps me to focus on what I've chosen to do and keeps me sane. Harry's trial is coming up next week. I just hope I'll be able to go through this without breaking down.

The adoption agency mentioned that I could probably just stick with their counseling, but Sherry and I are such good friends and I really don't want to leave her yet. That leaves Miss Crock at school and Mrs. Dora.

I talked to Mom and she agreed that we could let go of Mrs. Dora and Miss Crock. Mom will call both of them to explain the situation. Hopefully they'll agree I don't need to see them more than one last appointment. Yeah!

With all these appointments I'm starting to run out of time to study!

November 22nd

I have an appointment with the Adoption Worker tomorrow. I wanted to have Sherry there with me. She said she could come, but it might be better if I went alone. When I said that I would prefer if she came, she said okay, but that she wouldn't interfere with what the worker would suggest.

I asked her why she would hesitate and she said that sometimes girls want their counselor there to act as a referee instead of a friend. I looked at her and started laughing because it just struck me funny. Sherry *is* my friend!

She said she'd be glad to come at least once but when she checked her calendar she had an appointment scheduled for the same time.

Then you know what happened? Her phone rang and two of her clients canceled for tomorrow! Wow! When you pray to God, He moves mountains!

November 23rd

My worker is called Moira. She's quite nice and Sherry knows her. They chatted together for a bit. I told her the news that the doctor had said I was expecting twins.

You should have seen her face! Priceless! I'm still chuckling. It was so funny.

Mind you, I didn't feel like laughing right then. I mean, she could have said to get out and never come back or escorted me out the door to another room or person. I know God was there because He made me see the funny side of it. Sherry winked at me and said that whoever would adopt the two kids would be blessed.

Moira closed her mouth and then started smiling and then we all burst out laughing. It was so weird that we all three thought it funny!

Anyway, she said that she'd have to take my "Birthmother Application" and look it through again and come up with more matches.

Then she asked me this kind of funny question: What did I mean by wanting these two babies to be brought up in a Christian family?

I didn't have an answer for her, so she asked me to think about it. She'll let me call her for our next appointment.

I'm glad Sherry was with me. She hardly said a word during the whole hour, but it was like I had a friend with me, someone who can tell me what Moira said and remind me of anything I missed.

I've got enough stuff going on in my life right now with the trial coming up and school and these two beach balls. Will you two quit already?

I guess I never thought about it. Christian family. Mom is a Christian and so am I. But what did Moira mean?

November 24th

Mom and I sat down and talked about the question Moira asked me. She said that there are different kinds of religions and they were all Christian. I got her point. What we did was take a piece of paper and go through the Yellow Pages phone book and look up churches. They are listed under their denominations.

Do you know that there are Greek and Ukrainian Orthodox Churches and that they are different? Mom explained that by looking in the Yellow pages, I could see that there were different kinds of religions that all believed in the same things we did. It just depended on what I wanted my children to be raised by.

There's like the Alliance Church and the Anglicans, and the Catholics, and the Presbyterians, and the Mennonites and so on.....

There are a gazillion churches and denominations! Plus, there's something that caught my eye. It's called Messianic Church.

Mom says that these Christians are Jewish people that believe that Jesus Christ resurrected and that they believe that He is the Son of God, their Messiah, but that they need to keep the laws of Moses and the traditions of their ancestors, the Jewish people, to reach Paradise.

I think that's really awesome. It means that you would know the basics of the Word and have the advantage of the open door to Heaven.

Mom also reminded me that some Christians are very hard line. For one thing, some denominations ask that the elect stand before a congregation to renounce their former life troubles such as drugs or alcohol habits. Others expect you to join the faith only if you are mentored by a couple for a year before you are accepted into the congregation.

I asked her why that would need to be addressed. I thought that God took us as his children no matter what we have done. But she smiled and said that man will always have rules and laws to protect them. She told me to check the book of Leviticus if I wanted to see what the Law of Moses was all about. Maybe I will later. Now I'm getting too tired to hold my eyes opened.

Maybe at the adoption agency some couples would have put down their preferences in that quarter. I'll have to ask.

Oh, by the way, I made an appointment to see Moira again. This time Mom will come with me. It's her day off.

November 26th

After meeting with Moira, Mom and I sat down in the Tropical Conservatory at Assiniboine Park. It's pretty quiet there and soothing. We discussed what had happened during the session. See, at the first meeting, I didn't get all the things that the lawyers of the agency would have to have filled out by Harry. One of them in particular is called "Notice To Birth Father" and could hold up the adoption.

When I asked her why, she said that if he refused to be a father, everything would proceed as I hoped. But if he contests his rights, the adoption process could be held up for a long time in the court system.

I got dizzy and really hot. Moira got me a cup of cold water and told me to take deep breaths. Then she said that although it was a tough pill to swallow, that I needed to know what was happening and to be ready for that eventuality.

Mom told me that we'd pray about the situation and let God decide the outcome.

I don't know how Harry could want to be a father! He's so cocky and such a rotten person! He'd be a horrible example to these two! Oh my! Here go the tears again!

November 27th

Moira called. She'll be setting up "Match Meetings" for me soon.

November 28th

What happens if these two babies never make it into the world? What if nobody wants them? It doesn't matter if the adoption agency thinks they have a match, they could be horrible parents! I want good parents for these two!

What if I get into a car accident and die? What happens to these two lives? What if I decide to keep them after all?

Tough questions! I've got a difficult week coming up too. Mrs. B asked if I would like to share some of the things I have to deal with, emotion wise, to the rest of the class, but I told her that I can't. I'm scared I'll start crying in font of everybody.

It's too hard! I realize, it could be cool to do that, but then I might get either pity or offensive behavior from the rest of the class. No. I don't think it's time for this yet.

Oh Lord Jesus! Here I go again! Crying for no reason whatsoever! Why am I so depressed?

November 29th

Mr. Hatlow (that's the lawyer the legal system appointed us. He'll represent me at the trial), keeps telling me that it won't be as bad as I think or feel. He says that what happened to me has happened to other girls and women and that I was very brave to charge Harry.

It's nice to know that I'm not the only one, but I do believe I might be the only one that has not one, but two kids from it!

He also told us that the trial comprises (I think that means "many parts all together") of a series of different steps. The first trial will be to see if the judge wants it to be a private one or public with a jury. A jury! I hope not!

Isn't it strange that yesterday I was "down in the dumps" as Mom says? I don't understand why I would even WANT to keep these babies! I know I couldn't raise them right!

I want to do more than just be on social assistance for the rest of my life! I want more than that for these two babies! They deserve love, caring and two parents who won't yell at them constantly. Who won't take their own frustrations out on them.

Moira said that I had made it very clear on the parenting form that what I was looking for were responsible, Christian parents for these two babies. She said that Harry needs to know I'm pregnant and that he is still, according to the law, their father.

Why would these babies want him for a father? He's mean and a liar and hurtful and cruel!

I tried to tell that to Moira, but she was stubborn. She reminded me that she had talked about that eventuality at our first meeting.

I remember, but it doesn't make any sense to me. He assaulted me! He's the one that got me in this mess!

November 30th

Mom and I sat down last night and talked about what it was like for her to have me. She talked about the first three months of her pregnancy and said they were really tough because she had really BIG plans for her life.

When her boyfriend broke up with her, back in her hometown when she told him she was expecting me, she decided that she wasn't worth loving, that she was only a burden to those around her. Her boyfriend didn't want to get married or be ostracized from his family. Then he told her that he wasn't ready to be responsible for her mistake. (*HER mistake!* That's almost the same thing Harry told me!)

One of her friends had become pregnant two years earlier and had been forced to marry the man who was the father of her child. She said her mother had said that her friend had asked for the consequences of her actions and that she would be a 'shunned' woman for the rest of her life.

Mom said that it broke her friend's heart to find herself relegated on a farm, far from her family and friends and titled 'outcast' by the whole community.

I can't imagine it! It must have been awful! No wonder Mom left her family! But you know what made it even harder? She said her father had always told her that if she had been a boy, he would have given the farm over to her, but because she was the oldest of the family and a girl that she wasn't worth beans to him.

Imagine being told you were nothing! That must have hurt her so bad!

Now I know why Mrs. Dandeneau got all red and why Mom didn't want to talk to me about her childhood. No wonder she's so independent!

And to think that she had to put her dream of wanting to go to university and get a better education aside to take care of me! ME! And she even gave me my name. She called me Christina, because it reminded her of the love Jesus gave her when she needed it most.

Boy, it sure was tough listening to her tell me that! How could she be a burden to others? She's such a nice person and I haven't been very nice to her in the last two years. First with Charlotte and then with Harry.

I couldn't see that she was trying to protect me from them. Just goes to show that adults make mistakes too and that they've got close to a decade of experience more than we do.

So, I told her that. She gave me a hug and said that's how she was before she had God in her life. Told me that she often hated her parents, but that she thought she knew better than them. She said she thought she loved her boyfriend enough to marry him, but had come to realize much later on that their relationship wouldn't have been strong enough to stand together. That although he had forced her to abandon herself to the lust of sex and she had fought against his pressure, that he'd won in the end. She said that I needed to remember that I was the best thing that happened to her.

Mom mentioned that she felt ashamed and didn't want to be labeled like her friend, so she left her parents' house as soon as possible after the assault and the breakup of their relationship and moved to the city.

She found out just how tough it is to live in a big city with no support. She said she could have gone on assistance, but if you knew my mom, you'd know that she's pretty proud and she doesn't like charity. The only thing and job she'd had in the country was waitressing at the country pub, so she continued on with that.

When she found out she was pregnant, she had a choice to make: keep or give me away. Abortion was not an option for her, it wasn't even an option period! It was illegal when she got pregnant with me and there weren't any doctors she trusted to go see for one or even felt it was a right choice for her. She didn't want to see me raised in a family she didn't know and she couldn't see living in the same village that had ousted her friend.

Isn't it weird that I feel the same? Sherry says that with the adoption agency, they let me meet the potential parents. If Mom had had that chance, maybe I would have been raised by someone else.

Woah! Back-up and freeze!

Is that how these kids are going to feel about me? Will they feel like I'm abandoning them to strangers? Will they hate me for my decision? Will I-

No! Stop it! I have to stop thinking like this! I can't and won't keep the twins! I can't, can't, can't! Oh wow! Here I go crying again! Will I ever get over this?

I have to, because I want these two to have better luck than me. I've grown up with just a mom. I'd really like it if these two had a dad. I didn't. Maybe if I had one, I'd be a better, more balanced person. Maybe I'd have had an example of how to deal with men.

It's sad...... really.... because I'll never know.

December 4th

Tomorrow is the pre-trial. I have to be at the courthouse by nine. I'm nervous. I don't know if I'll be calm. Just seeing Harry is going to be tough.

I remember Mrs. Dora saying that it's important that I face him to start grieving our relationship properly. Sherry said that I'm a strong person that I can do this and to remember that I'm not alone, that God is with me, wherever I am.

I also need to remember that Harry is stalling on the "Notice to Birth Father". I sure hope he gives up his rights. I'm praying and so is Mom. What would he want with two kids? He'd be a horrible father!

December 5th

I'll tell you later what happens. These kids know something's up, because they haven't stopped moving this morning. Ouch! Settle down there # 1, you're going to make your surrogate mother chuckle during court. Why can't you be like # 2? He's quiet and simply stretches.

Mr. Hatlow really wants me to concentrate on his left hand. He says that when I'll see his index finger going up and down, that I'm to take two deep breaths and let them out slowly.

He says that what will happen today is not a real court day. It's a time when the two sides meet with the judge and decide if a jury and trial is necessary. Some evidence will be presented, but it will be mostly what the lawyers have gathered in cross-examining their clients. I am only to answer if the judge asks me a direct question. Mr. Hatlow will answer all the other ones.

I hope the judge doesn't ask me anything!

2 p.m.

We're still in the courthouse, but outside the courtroom. That's why I can write in here. I really want to tell you what happened this morning, but there's too many people around and Mr. Hatlow says that I need to stay focused for the final stage of today.

8 p.m.

We got out of the court at around five thirty and I'm shaky still. Would you believe Harry denied he ever hurt me? Would you believe he tried to make the judge believe that I had consented to having sex with him? That I was lying? That I was the one who had initiated the actions and that he was the victim and not me?

And you know the worst? He accused me of sicking a lawyer on him to bind him down by telling him I was pregnant!!!

I can't believe he was such a manipulator and that I didn't see it!

He just doesn't see that he's done anything wrong! I had to sit today and listen to what he had to say and it was a good thing Mr. Hatlow was there, because whenever Harry said something that wasn't the truth, he put a hand on the table and tapped his index flat.

I thought that my 'case' as Mr. H calls it, wouldn't need a jury, but the judge ruled otherwise. He said it would be much better and the two lawyers agreed! Don't they know that Mom and I can't afford a lot of expensive things like this? I mean, Mom checked on the Internet at work and we found out that it costs about a thousand dollars a day on a trial! What are we going to do?

Mom said she'd talk it over with Mr. H and he told her today that he'd have her come in to his office to discuss this later.

So now, I wait. Mom waits. We all wait. This is going to be murder!

It could be.... what did Mr. H call it? Re-something.....

Oh well, I'm so tired tonight, what with an essay on 'English Literature at the turn of the Twentieth Century', that I'm going to need all my energy to concentrate on this until I go to bed. Yawn! My bed looks more inviting than ever.

December 6th

Would you believe the opening trial has been set to start two weeks before Christmas? That's like really making me and Mom happy! Couldn't they wait until after the New Year?

I have an appointment with Mr. H tomorrow. I'm going to talk this over with him. Two weeks before Christmas - I'm in EXAMS!!!!!

I saw Moira today. She said that since I had finished filling in my potential parents list that there are a few couples that might be interested.

Let's hope one of them and I make a hit.

December 7th

Mr. Hatlow says that he can't change the date! I went back to school and talked with Mrs. B who said that I could take all my exams a week before.

That's next week !!!!!

I've got to cram all that info into my head in six days! How am I going to do this with sleep disturbed nights, walking every time these two cramp me up and staying on top of everything?

Oh, why can't I just have been like others and let everything slide? Couldn't I have just refused to take Harry to court? Tears again!

Why me? Why did this have to happen to me? I feel so alone, so stuck.... no, more like rejected.

Yeah, rejected. Good word. Is there anybody out there that understands what I'm going through?

10 p.m.

Mom and I had a good talk. She said: "Teena. Everyone, at one point in their life, feels like you do. We'd like to have a magic wand and just wipe everything away. Unluckily, or even maybe luckily, reality is that God has the ultimate control over the course and path of our lives. He loves us too much to send us more than we can handle." I guess, to a certain point, I'm being selfish. So God wants me to stretch a bit. Okay fine, but what do I do when these feelings take over? It's like I can't control myself anymore!

I guess I just have to remember that little extra Mom added. "Sometimes God allows bad things to happen to us because He has a better ending in sight. If we didn't go through the bad stuff, we wouldn't grow through them and become better persons."

Reading over the last entry I understand that God is trying to do something in me. But is it wrong to want the pain to go away in a snap? Mom just hugged me and said that that was what growing up was all about. Learning to live with the punches and parties.

December 9th

I'm not doing too bad, but not the greatest. I saw Dr. Ross today and he says that I've now finished my second trimester and that the babies are growing well. He wanted to send me for another ultrasound in two weeks but when I told him about the trial, he stopped writing and turned to me.

He asked how I felt about all these changes and struggles. Do you know that I started crying? Talk about embarrassing!

But he smiled so nicely at me, like he really cares what happens to me! Me! A girl that's pregnant and so mixed up! He said that it was okay to cry, that it was a natural release of pent-up emotions. And then he patted me on the shoulder and said that now I'd feel a lot better.

He's right, I feel a lot better just knowing that he knows what I'm going through. He still wants me to go for the ultrasound, but he said that I was to call his office after the opening trial and he'd try to get me in between trial times.

10 p.m.

Mom just stopped by my room on her way in from work. She says her prayers have been answered. I asked her which one, as she seems to pray for me a lot lately. Said that she's been praying for an understanding doctor, one that would not put me down over my choices or feelings and emotions.

God? If You can really hear me, make sure that these two babies will get good, kind, loving Christian parents. That they'll love these two kids like their own. Help me Father, to know You better. Help me to get past these bad feelings. Help me through this trial. Help these two babies understand that I'm giving them to loving parents, not that I'm abandoning them. Amen.

December 14th

I've done English Lit, Français, Math 4 and Biology. Now I'm free! Free! Yeah!

Well, sort of... the opening trial is on Monday. I have an appointment with Mr. H. tomorrow morning. He wants to make sure that he, Mom and I know exactly what to expect and also to go over a few pointers.

December 15th

Do you know that I can't wear jeans at the courthouse? Mom and I had to go shopping for a dress. Me in a dress!!! Talk about feeling weird. I haven't worn a skirt and heels since THAT night!!

I'm kind of a bit bigger in front. Mom took me to a place that sells both baby and maternity clothes and I had to really steel my heart to focus on what we were shopping for. Mom caught on pretty quick that I didn't feel comfortable in the store. She grabbed my hand and we went back into the car.

"I'm sorry honey. I just didn't think."

She's hurting as much as me I think. We ended up at our favorite boutique. The Diabetic Association's thrift shop, our 'V V Boutique' as Mom calls it and found a simple dress and shoes. At least I don't feel like a granny or a fat, pregnant, bag lady. Mom laughed when I told her that. She said that her daughter was a beautiful, special young woman who amazed her by her zest for life and was making choices that were right for her.

She's so amazing herself! Sometimes she floors me with her understanding!

December 17th

Talk about tough! There are twelve people in the jury box! Six men and six women. Some of them are really old (at least to me they are). One of the men has white hair and he looks just like a grandpa.

Mom sat in the benches behind me. Mr. Hatlow said that I had to do this on my own from the start, otherwise I'd see her as my crutch. I didn't agree with him, but now I think I understand his point of view because throughout the day I just wanted to grab a hold of her and have her arms around me. He said that the jury needed to see that I was mature enough to stand on my own if need be.

Mr. H said he was proud of me today, because I followed his guidance. He says the jurors are on my side. (I sure hope so!)

It's helped that I saw Harry a few weeks ago too because now I'm used to, well...sort of.... his presence in the same room as me.

Mr. H also told me that if I needed some time off for a doctor's appointment to get it done after the court time, after five. So I'll have to call Dr. Ross's office tonight or maybe early tomorrow morning. It's going to be Christmas next week!

He also says that the judge might postpone the trial until the New Year to give the jurors a Christmas break.

Mrs. B said that I'll get the results of my exams when I come back in class after the Christmas break! That's a long time to wait, but I can't really ask for anything more.

Sherry wants to see me whenever I feel I need to talk about what's going on and Nic said that she'd be praying for me. She also said that I can call her whenever I feel that I need to talk to someone, no matter what time it is! (I hope her parents don't mind.)

It's nice to know so many people care about me.

December 21st

I know it's only a few days before Christmas, but I called Sherry. Just talking to her on the phone helped me a lot. We talked about what I was feeling, how the babies were behaving.

Moira called and said that the adoption agency is willing to wait until the trial is done before inviting me to visit their office. Apparently they have five couples interested. Woooowee!!!

December 24th

It's a tradition in the French-Canadian families to go to Midnight Mass. For Mom and me, we don't go to a Catholic service; we go to a Non-Denominational church. Their service is earlier in the evening and it's a candlelight service.

There are no lights on anywhere, just candles burning in the sanctuary and around where we sit. The musicians have discreet book lights on their stands.

They sing praise and worship songs for about twenty minutes, then switch to popular and well known Christmas hymns. Then our pastor comes up and talks about the reason why Jesus Christ came to Earth.

Do you know that tonight I felt a bit like Mary felt? Here she was carrying a baby that her husband hadn't fathered. Almost like these two. Joseph was a brave man to accept to be Jesus' father.

But the nicest thing about Jesus' coming is that He opened a door for all of us. By becoming human, he was able to understand where we stand and how we fail so very often. Like me.

I don't want to keep these two babies because deep down I know I'm too young to look after them, but I'm making sure that they will have a home that's just right for them instead of a home life that would probably be traumatic and unsafe. Not that Mom and I would mistreat them, but we don't have the financial security to be able to provide for them. I don't have the emotional maturity to handle two babies!

Sometimes I wish that they could stay, that I could keep them..... but then I remember Monster and the night I wanted to put him in the garage to not have to deal with his constant crying or the so many times I yelled at the doll to try and shut him up! I could one day shake the life out one of these babies and kill them!

Lord, thank You that You are keeping me sane in all this, for keeping me on track. Thank you for sending Your son to Earth. Amen.

Christmas Day!

Isn't it amazing that three years ago, Mom gave me you? I thought I'd never write anything in you or on your pages. And look at you now! Awesome!

Mom has always had this day off. The bar doesn't open on Christmas Day and she refuses to work her other jobs too. We get to spend the morning in bed relaxing.....aaaaah!

Now, if only these two would understand the concept of relaxation... will you quit hitting each other? You're going to hurt yourselves!

Mom always comes in during the night to attach a long sock on the end of my bed, but I caught her this time! I was awake when she snuck in, but I didn't let on.

There's always the neatest things in there. One year I got a potato at the bottom of the sock because we didn't have enough money to buy mandarin oranges. This year, I'm pretty sure there's a mandarin at the bottom. A sign that financially, Mom is doing fairly well. Or is she? I wonder what I'll get this time.

6 p.m.

I've just woken up from a good nap. It's amazing to me that even though I have lots of energy most days, right now I feel drained and tired. Mom says it might have a lot to do with the stress of the trial. I guess she's right.

Anyway, guess what I got for Christmas? Mom bought me this most beautiful Bible. The cover is like a paperback and we'll cover it with plastic protector later tonight. The version is a New International and it's pretty easy to read.

10 p.m.

Mom has to work tomorrow so I'll have the house to myself. I called Nic and she'll be coming over. It will be a lot of fun just gabbing to our hearts content!

December 26th

I had the greatest day! Nic and two of our other friends came over and we had a small party. We talked about....guess.... guys, of course! What else are we going to talk about?

Nic got her long hair cut short and does she ever look good! I never knew just cutting your hair could do that.

But now I'm really tired and it's barely eight in the evening. I told Nic that I had a great time, but that I needed to go to bed before I fell asleep on them. Mom and I agreed that if I was tired that I needed to ask my friends to leave if she wasn't home.

Not that Mom doesn't trust my friends... well, at least my girl friends. It's better this way, but anything could happen, right?

December 29th

I saw Mrs. Dora for my last appointment today. I told her that the adoption agency has appointed me an adoption worker and that I have to drop one counselor at least. She said that I could always come back to see her after, that if I remembered, Mom had put me with her right after the assault and that sometimes it works and sometimes it doesn't.

I said that I wasn't angry at her or anything and she reassured me.

"Teena, when there are too many cooks in the kitchen, the soup get too salty."

We laughed and I said that she was probably right, but it was just that I didn't want to hurt her feelings. She said that I wasn't, that it was bound to happen soon and that she was glad that she had been able to help me.

She told me that I'm growing up faster than she ever thought I would. That I'm getting my life under control and that I'm starting to make decisions.

She cautioned me too. She said that whatever I learn this year, that it will have a profound impact on the rest of my life. Well, duh!

Of course she went on to say that sometimes when the girls she's counseled get over the delivery of their babies they go back to how they were before they got pregnant.

That won't happen to me, I told her and she just looked at me with those owl eyes of hers and said that she believed me.

"You're different than the others. You have the drive to make the best decision possible to ensure that those two children have a chance at life with a family that loves them and gives them what you can't: a stable, peaceful and growing family."

If only Harry had been a nice guy. Maybe it could have worked out for us. We could have gotten married and kept these two..... not! If Dora was here she'd tell me to take off my shades and she'd be right.

There's no sense wishing for something that isn't going to happen. Harry's made up his mind about me. If he wants to blame me for the whole thing, that's his position. I'm the victim. He's the abuser. I am not ever going to fall in that trap again! I just hope he doesn't stall much longer on the Birth Father's Rights document. I'm getting nervous. What would he want with two babies? What could he possibly want with such responsibility? He always told me that he liked his freedom!

January 3rd

Mom said that I was really special to her today. I've always been a daughter to her, but why am I special only now? You know what she said?

"You're special because you have so much more courage than I did and I'm proud of you. You'll make something out of your life, you just wait and see. "

Wow! Sometimes she just comes out with stuff in a way that I have nothing to answer her with.

January 6th

Every year, Mom and I have some friends over for Epiphany Night. That's really the day that the three wise men came to visit Jesus. It's a special evening where we bless our guests with good food, good fellowship and gifts.

Mom and I don't buy gifts for them, we take things of our own that we have in the house and give them away. She says that it is in blessing others with our own belongings that makes God happy. I asked her why and she said that God has asked us to leave everything behind and follow Him. If we stay attached to all our material things, then we can't follow him.

She showed me the passage in the Bible about the rich and wealthy man who asked Jesus what he needed to do to enter into the kingdom of God. Jesus told him that he needed to sell all his possessions and leave his house to follow him. The man couldn't do that because he loved his possessions too much. Then she told me about Zaccheus.

He was a very short man and when he heard that Jesus was coming to his hometown, he ran ahead and climbed into a tree so that he'd be able to see Him. When Jesus saw him up in the tree, he told him to come down, that he was going to be staying at his house for the night.

Zaccheus was truly happy and they went home together. When he asked Jesus what he could do to follow him, Jesus said that he had to sell and leave everything behind him. Zac said he'd give away half of all his wealth and four times what he owed to those he had wronged, because he couldn't leave his father's estate.

Mom says that sometimes we are like that rich man, thinking that we need to have the best shoes or the best clothes or the best of everything. Like when all I wanted for Christmas was a Rocawear sweatshirt. There can be a selfish part in all of us that wants to keep those things of our past close to our heart. More like hanging on to the anger against someone who's hurt us. Instead, we need to do like Zaccheus and give four times away what we owe them, in a loving way so that we don't hold grudges.

Just like the grudge I have against Harry.

I'm sitting here thinking about that grudge. Why shouldn't I be angry with him? He's ruined my life! He's taken my body and turned it into something that I never dreamed it would be! And I don't want these two to have an angry mother! Plus I don't want them to know that their father is a serial rapist either!

Midnight

I learned something tonight. Mom gave away the crystal vase that she got years ago for her birthday. One of her friends had gotten it for her. Do you know that she gave it to Henriette?

You should have been there! She started crying when she opened her gift! Henriette said she'd never seen anything so beautiful in all her life! She wrapped her arms around Mom and even I had tears in my eyes.

Mom never really used it, I guess. She's the practical type and a canning jar works just as well as a crystal vase. Mark got a Hardy Boys book that Mom picked out of the garbage after our neighbor had his garage sale last summer. Mark said he hadn't got that one.

I wonder how Mom knows what each person needs? It's uncanny! Roger was really surprised when he opened his gift. It came from my room. A long time ago, I think I was in grade five; I made a cross with two sticks and some raffia for an Easter project. I don't need a cross to remind me of Jesus anymore, because He lives in my heart. When he opened his gift, he looked at Mom and said that he'd never seen anything so beautiful! Amazing!

I start school tomorrow. I'm "showing" much more now (that means my stomach sticks out more and I look pregnant). Back to the torture room in a few days too. I hope the judge will give Harry more than just a slap on the wrist. Mr. Hatlow said that he could get up to 4 years in jail. I hope he gets more!

January 10th

Today's the big day! The day when the two sides will present the physical evidence. Things like the crime scene and the medical examination results. Mr. H said that the judge will ask me why I refused to take the "morning after pill" and he said that I was just to tell the judge and jury what I told him when he asked me the same question.

I'm swallowing here. What if I had taken that pill? What if I had killed these two babies? I wouldn't have been able to live with that decision! No matter how much I know that I can't be a good parent, no matter what anyone else says, I can't kill someone else.

Sherry showed me a really important verse in the Bible when I saw her last time. It says that God creates each one of us before we are born. That's in Psalm 139 starting at verse 13 to 19. I found the verse today because I'll need that extra strength from God today. It says: "For you created my inmost being; you knit me together in my mother's womb. (...)" Then it says:

"My frame (that's my bones and organs), was not hidden from you when I was made in the secret place (that's the uterus). When I was woven together in the depths of the earth (that's even BEFORE we are created!), your eyes saw my unformed body. (That is so amazing! That's saying that God sees us created even before we are created in our mother's womb, before we get pregnant and before we are born! That's awesome!.... It's so cool!) When I awake I am still with you." (That means that when we are born, we still belong to God.)

Mom has an Amplified Bible and it has different words for this psalm, but it means the same thing... I just find that the words are nicer.

"For You did form my inward parts; You did knit me together in my mother's womb. (...) My frame was not hidden from you when I was being formed in secret and intricately and curiously wrought, as if embroidered with various colors in the depths of the earth, a region of darkness and mystery. Your eyes saw my unformed substance, and in Your book, all the days of my life were written before ever they took shape, when as yet there was none of them."

So, no. I couldn't take a pill to erase what God had already formed before I knew it. I couldn't destroy His plan for my life. I remember now what I told Mr. H: "Maybe I'll be wiser through this. I know I'll be different."

8 p.m.

I'm exhausted! These babies haven't stopped moving around all evening! They know something's up. I just hope I can get some sleep!

The doctor who examined me in the Emergency said that I had been very adamant (that's stubborn in Mom's vocabulary) about not taking the pill. Harry's lawyer asked why and the doctor said that it was against my human beliefs.

Human belief! It's more than that! It's plain religious beliefs! Who would have thought that the doctor had to be politically correct in a court room where they ask you to *swear to tell the truth, nothing but the truth, so help me God?*

The doctor presented the pictures of me that the Emergency people took when I was in there after the assault. (Thank goodness he didn't show them to me!)

Mr. H asked the doctor if there was any way that I could have faked the sexual assault. The doctor said that there was no mistake and he went on to state the physical medical evidence.

As he talked, that day came rushing back.

Mom's arms around me, me crying my eyes out, the doctor poking in places that weren't comfortable, really hurt, places that Harry left his... whatever on. Me knowing that my life was never going to be the same again.

At the lunch break, the doctor stopped beside me and told me that I was very brave standing up for what had happened to me.

Mr. H had to put up his finger a few times today. He told me that I was doing well, but that I needed to remember to keep quiet while he examined the witnesses.

Tomorrow, the detective and the Victims Bureau will present their side of the case.

God? Help me out tonight! Calm these two babies that You have formed in me so that I can at least sleep tonight. Amen.

January 11th

I'm crossing my fingers because today the Sex Crime Unit will be bringing all the exhibits. I just hope that this time Harry won't try to blame everything on me.

9:30 p.m.

It was not easy to see the pictures of the crime scene that the female detective brought out. Mr. H held my hand under the table when I started getting all shaky. It felt good to know that he understands that this was really hard for me.

Exhibit A - as the detective said, was the scene of the assault. Do you know that when she showed those pictures of my torn shirt I started crying? Mr. Hatlow had to pass me a tissue because I couldn't stop crying. It brought so much of that night back that I was scared beyond belief. And I thought listening to the doctor was bad! I thought that I'd be okay too, because I did go back to the scene with the Victim's Bureau, remember? But this was harder. A lot harder. Maybe the other time was easier because it was outside with birds chirping. This was so ... oh, I don't know.... cold, unfeeling.

I know it's important to bring Harry to justice, but does it mean that I have to stay through all the trial? I asked Mr. Hatlow why I had to be there for the day and he said that it was important that I remember what he had told me before we went to trial. "You need to acknowledge that what happened did, that what you lived through that night was real and that others saw what happened. It's the only way that you'll be able to recover from this."

I know he's right, but it's really tough just sitting there and reliving the whole horrid night!

It doesn't help that these two babies are moving in my abdomen like two beach balls hitting the walls of the gym!

Settle down you two!

3 a.m.

I haven't slept a wink! These two are driving me up the wall! They haven't stopped bouncing and stretching all night!

Mom is taking some time off of work to be with me this week. She says she wants to be there for me. She keeps telling me that I'm really brave and that I'm doing the right thing. I don't feel very brave right now. I feel claustrophobic! It's as if Harry is trying to fence me in again. Trying to make me believe that it's all in my head that what he did to me wasn't anything out of the ordinary.

God, please help me out with this! Keep me strong and able to go on. Help me not cry in the courtroom and hold me up because I feel as though I'm coming apart! Help Mom, because I think she's reliving part of what happened to her. I hear her crying in her room these past few nights. Be with her and take care of her.

Amen.

January 12th

We got out of court early today because there was a fire in the cafeteria kitchen of the law courts. So I asked Mr. H if it was all right to go to school. He said it was okay, but he wondered why I wanted to. He also told me that I needed to exercise caution in not mentioning too much of the proceedings as each trial is different for every case. Actually, each trial is confidential unless publicized by the medias, which ours isn't.

Mom caught up to us then and said that there was no question of me going to school. She was taking me out to lunch instead and then shopping for a few more clothes that she wanted me to have.

I had to stop Mom from buying me anything. She can't afford any extras for me. She wanted to take me to an expensive restaurant as a special treat, but I told her that if she really wanted to take me out, that the cafeteria at school was good enough. She laughed and said that wasn't what she had in mind.

We finally ended up at a self-serve buffet where I'm ashamed to say I stuffed my face! I sure hope this keeps up! I haven't been able to keep much food down the past few months and now it's like I can't stop eating!

January 13th

Today was interesting to say the least. Now that the jurors have the 'hard evidence', (that's the evidence that is see-able... I hope that's a word), they need to hear the two parties' evidence. That's mine and Harry's.

Mr. H. asked the judge prior to the trial if I could go before Harry, but the judge said that it would be the luck of the draw that would work in our case. I don't know who will go first yet. I'll find out tomorrow. I'm praying that I'll go first.

Which reminds me of the cops that park behind our house. You know they sent me a bouquet of flowers yesterday? There was a card too! (I'm putting it in here.)

Mom said: "You see Teena, it's not everyone that thinks that you made a mistake. These men see a lot more hurting people and youths than we could even think! It's actually a sign that they are on your side."

January 14th

God came through! I'm first. We got a call from Mr. H last night. Today's the big day.

I know You will be with me today, so please guard my tongue, because I'm afraid I'll say something wrong.

It's my turn to tell what happened. Mr. H said that I have to be really careful what I say and how I say it, because Harry's lawyer is going to try to trip me up every chance he gets. So, please Lord, be my guide and shelter.

9 p.m.

Sitting in the witness's bench is sort of like sitting down for an exam. The judge is on your left, a little higher and a bit behind you. The lawyers sit in front of you at long tables, usually with whatever files they need for their client's case and their client sits on either their left or right depending on which table they are sat at by the sheriffs (they are the ones that call the court 'to order', which is when we stand when the judge comes in every day). The jury sits in a sort of elevated box on the left of the witness's chair, which is on the other side of the 'judge's bench' as the unit I sat in is called.

I tried really hard not to be intimidated by Harry sitting next to his lawyer. I'm glad Mr. Hatlow made me practice this, because it really helped me. He said I had to bring the judge into my answers, that I needed to include Harry and himself too. That was hard!

Mom sits in the row of chairs two down from where I am with my lawyer. She smiled at me when I sat in the witness's box. Mr. H. said that she needed to remember to be quiet and not distract me, so that she wouldn't influence me.

Sigh. It's really hard to do something when you know that your best supporter has to be silent.

Mom said it was the hardest thing she's ever done. She said that she wished she'd been able to be out in the hall or in another room so that she wouldn't have to stop herself from getting up and putting her arms around me.

I know she was praying because once in a while I could see her lips moving.

When Harry's lawyer came up to me, I sent a look to Mr. H and he tapped his finger on the table twice. That helped me to relax and I looked at the man across from me. I guess the comment that Mr. H. said yesterday stuck.

"The other lawyer is just another man like me. We have to press forward to make sure that all the evidence is laid out for all to see. If it means that we get it by asking questions or by presenting an exhibit to the court, then that's what we do. The important thing to remember is to speak the truth. Don't let yourself get flustered. Take a deep breath and let it out slowly. Concentrate on the person asking you questions. Look at the judge, the lawyer and Harry before answering. " Then he smiled and said I was a strong person and that I could do this.

Mr. H really helps me understand that I don't need to feel intimidated by anyone in the courtroom. Well, except the judge.

The other lawyer asked me to describe how Harry brought me to those woods. Then he tried to make me agree that Harry had simply given me what I had been begging for. He tried to trip me up, but I told him the truth and he had to abstain from a few questions. The judge is really good. I'm hoping that tomorrow I won't be asked to get back up there.

Mom might be asked to testify on Monday. We don't know yet. Because it was longer than twenty four hours before she brought me to the Emergency, the judge wants to understand why she didn't check on me that night.

Mom is nervous, I think. "You looked so calm and collected up there, Christina. I'm hoping I'll be as brave."

I told her that I just followed Mr. H's suggestions. She smiled at me and gave me a hug.

At least we've got the weekend to prepare. Mr. H wants Mom to come to his office tomorrow morning so that he can help her prepare for the trial. I know he will. He's really good at helping me.

January 15th

Would you believe that Mom came back from Mr. H's office with a smile on her lips? She said that he was a very nice man who understood where she was coming from.

I wonder what that means.

January 17th

Mom is on the stand today. She says she's nervous, but I know she'll do well. She always does.

8 p.m.

I am so tired, it's not even funny. I can't wait until this trial is over so that I can get on with my life. It's so hard to just stay sane. On the one hand there's the trial. On the other, the adoption, the doctor's visits, the meetings, the ultrasounds and the whole other stuff that is driving me *crazy!*

Mom was awesome this morning! When Harry's lawyer cross-examined her and said that she had neglected me because she'd not found out I was alone in my bedroom for two days, she just about snapped his head off! Harry's lawyer kept trying to paint her black!

Mr. Hatlow called for an objection and it was the judge that asked her to explain the circumstances. She did and the judge took notes. I'm not sure if this will make a difference in the case.

Even the judge and jurors can't fault her with what she told them. Laura's labor started before I came home and when Harry's lawyer asked why she hadn't checked to make sure I was home when she came back, she said that I hadn't put on any lights in my room. She thought I was over at Nic's.

He can't fault her for that, can he?

After the other was done, Mr. H turned to the jury and asked if they, as parents hadn't also had times when they had not known that their children were home. He asked them if they recalled a time when their teenagers didn't have their radios on full blast. Some of the jurors chuckled, like the old grandpa.

I have to admit Mr. H is right. When I'm home, the radio is on too loud. I asked Mom if it bothered her and she said it didn't really. She said she'd be more worried now if she knew I was home and it wasn't on or that I had another station on.

We agreed that if ever I'm in trouble to switch the radio station to a classical one so that she'll know I need help. Hey! Maybe I'll do that when I go into labor!

January 18th

Today it's Harry's turn. *God, please keep me calm.*

10 p.m.

I know I'm supposed to be asleep right now, but Mom and I sat up tonight just discussing what happened today. She says that Harry's the type of man that cannot accept responsibility for his actions and that he reminded her of my father.

I asked if he and she had loved each other at one time. Mom just looked at me and, well.... her eyes were wet! I apologized and she hugged me and said it was okay to ask. "You're his daughter too, Teena."

He wasn't a very responsible kind of man. That many times he blamed others for his own mistakes. She said that she tried really hard to help me make wise decisions growing up and that she was very proud of me.

I guess when you try hard enough, you get results. It's strange to see how much I've changed since Harry assaulted me. I used to be so dependent on other people to be who I am.

Remember how I used to think that if Charlie was my friend that I was part of her crowd and part of something? That I was a valuable something, a something more than I had been before? I've learned since meeting Harry that I was an 'enabler', that is to say someone who lets another do to him or her what he wants instead of standing firm on truth and not budging. Actually, I stopped being Harry's enabler when I refused to take the Morning After Pill. I took responsibility for my body and these two's lives.

Now I'm starting to realize that I *can* be a person. I might not be wise yet, but I'm getting better at feeling okay about who I am.

January 19th

Mr. H told me that he didn't know who Harry's lawyer would call as a witness. He did say that he was able to track the cab driver that took me home. The cab driver! That reminds me that he didn't even accept my emergency money that night!

9 p.m.

After a full day I'm tired. So tired, I can hardly keep my eyes open. I'll write tomorrow morning.

January 20th

The cab driver's testimony was really important! I saw the way the jury looked at him and took him seriously.

The poor man looked like he was going to cry on the stand. Remember he wouldn't even take money for the ride? He said that he couldn't, that I reminded him of his own daughter at my age the night she had been killed.

The judge had the weirdest look on his face! He said that they would recess until tomorrow. Then the cab driver, Mr. Peterson, left the court room and Mr. H said that he'd known that something like this would happen.

He said he was glad that Mr. Peterson had been the one to pick me up that night. I asked him why, but Mr. H didn't answer me. He just said to wait. I wonder why?

January 21st

Mr. Peterson is back on the witness stand today. I wonder what he still has to say.

7 p.m.

The cab driver.... well.... Turns out that he is a retired lawyer who works as a cab driver because he doesn't want to stay home alone. He likes what he does. He doesn't have any grandchildren, which is really too bad. He'd be a really nice grandfather to have.

When Mr. H asked him what he had been before, the cab driver looked at the judge with a twinkle in his eyes and said that he'd been what the judge had been before he was appointed.

I'm off here. Mr. Peterson said he was glad that God had sent him to answer my call, because he really understood that night what I was going through, but that he respected me enough to not push me into doing something that I didn't want to do, like going to the hospital on my own.

Harry's lawyer tried to trip him up on that comment, but Mr. Peterson stared him down and said that anyone seeing the pictures of what I looked like two days later hadn't seen what I had looked like that night.

Did you know that there are video cameras in taxis? He had the cab company keep the video clip. Mr. H had arranged for a DVD player for the court room and they ran the sequence for the jury.

When I saw myself, I started shaking – *hard*. I had no idea how bad I looked! My hair was all over the place, my bloodied camisole was even worse! I thought looking at the crime scene was shocking enough. This was ten times worse! It took me a long time to stop feeling overwhelmed.

I don't think I had any circulation in my hands during the whole of the clip! Just thinking about it still makes me really shaky! Mom had tears running down her face! *Thank you God for sending Mr. Peterson! He was exactly what I needed.*

Monday, it will be the turn of the two lawyers to address the jury.

I wonder what Mr. H is going to say and what Harry's lawyer will say?

The jury is going to be behind closed doors for the weekend. That means that they won't have any contact with their families. That must be really tough.

January 24th

Remember how I was the first to give my testimony? That meant that the last comments of the trial would be delivered by the lawyers in the reverse order. That means Harry's lawyer was first. He got up and told the jury that his client was an innocent bystander that had been roped in by my obvious juvenile scheming, that I had lured him into believing that I could handle what he eventually had no choice but to give me - sexual intercourse. That what I believed to be the sequence of events of that night held more of a phantasmagorical series of photos in my mind than reality. The wooded area I had described was nothing more than fantasy on my part.

That I had goaded him into buying me the clothes that I wore that night. Then he added that I was simply a young woman who always got what she asked for. Just because his client was being tried here in Winnipeg, didn't mean that he had to stay here and have a constant reminder that a young, immature girl that had a mother that worked in bars, and who knew what kind of influence that had had on my life, had tricked him into doing an act that was not on his client's agenda. The judge stopped him at the comment about Mom's work and the man had to retract his comment. But I think the damage was done. Mom is a lot more than just a waitress in a bar! She's a very responsible person who has done the best she could to raise me and as a responsible citizen too.

It's a good thing that Mr. H held my hand under the table this time because I wanted to leap up and throttle Harry. Never mind Harry. I wanted to strangle his lawyer for saying those hurtful things about Mom!

The whole time Harry's lawyer was talking to the jury, Harry sat bent forward in his chair and looked like a victim. *The villain! The hypocrite!*

Mr. H talked about the whole thing from start to finish. He asked the jury four questions:

What would they have wanted me to do differently? What, in their opinion, would have been the best course to take? Why was Harry denying that he'd ever caused me any grief in the face of the hard evidence and witness accounts that had been presented in the court trial? And why was Harry also denying that he had never done anything like this to anyone else when the police had told the court in the beginning of the trial that Harry was wanted in other provinces for the sexual assault of other young women?

After the jury filed out, Mr. H and I sat down with Mom outside the courtroom for a few minutes. He said that it might take the jury a few hours or even a few days before they came up with a sentence of guilty or not guilty.

Because it was almost four thirty by the time we finished in court today, the judge said that the jury would deliberate behind closed doors until they had reached a verdict, then the court would reconvene tomorrow morning.

I wonder what he'll get?

January 25th

Today's the day when I find out what's going to happen. Will we win?

10 p.m.

Would you believe only two years? *TWO YEARS!!!* He is to have no contact with me and he's also to go for a trial in Saskatoon later. Mr. Hatlow said that his lawyer probably had a lot to do with the sentence. He says that there is a possibility that the other trials will add more years in jail time. He could end up serving them at just one institution or at several.

He asked me if I felt better about the fact that Harry would not be bothering me anymore.

"He might not bother me anymore, but that until the two babies I'm carrying are not with their parents, I'll still have a part of Harry in me."

He smiled and said that he understood my anger, but that I needed to "remember that it's only a small part of him in you. Those babies are more a part of you than him." Then he said that as these two will be going to a couple, they would get the influence of their parents more than Harry. I guess he's got a point.

Mom has to wait until we get the bill from Mr. Hatlow for his services. I hope it will not be beyond Mom's budget.

PART THREE

Walking Towards Freedom – "For I know the
plans I have for you. Plans to encourage you and
prosper you. Not for evil, but for freedom."

A paraphrase of Jer 29:11

January 27th

I met with Moira today. She asked how I was doing with the trial being over and all that was going on with my emotions. I really haven't had the time to sit down and think about things. I'm still stuck with the fact that it's over, but I've still got part of him in me. It's like there's a jiggle toy in my stomach that hasn't stopped making noise since he assaulted me. I guess it won't go away until these two are born.

Will you two just take it easy? I'm going for a glass of milk. Maybe that'll settle 'em down.

10 p.m.

Mom and I talked. In fact we've been talking a lot lately. There's so much going on! She asked how I really felt about having to let Mrs. Dora go. I don't really mind because Moira is so nice and patient with me. It's like she knows what's in my head even before I can say it. Sherry, when I go to see her, she's like an angel and she prays before and after each of our sessions. I'm glad that she can come once in a while to the adoption agency. It's like having a friend or even better, having Jesus beside me.

It's different when Mom is there. She asks all kinds of questions. I wonder if she wonders what would have happened if she'd given me up for adoption? Woah! Hold up!

What if I had been adopted? Would I have met Harry? Would I have had all that bad stuff happen with Charlotte? To think that I'd never have met Nic!

Oh God! What if I had been adopted? Will these two feel like that? Will they wonder why I sent, or rather gave them away? Will they blame me or hate me? Will they realize that I wasn't good enough to be their mother? Help me out! I feel as if there's this really heavy weight on my heart. Am I making the right decision? Or am I just fooling myself?

January 28th

Amazing! Two thousand dollars! That's how much Mom has to pay Legal Aid! She explained that they've put a lien on this house and if she can't finish paying it off that when she sells the house, a portion of the sale will go to clear her bill. That sounds crazy to me! It's as if the government was acting like the Mafia! *'Pay up or we get your house!'*

February 1st

I'm halfway and a bit. Dr. Ross is happy with my progress. He says that he wants me to have an ultrasound once a month from now on, just to make sure everything is going well. He also said that I'm doing better weight-wise and that the babies are growing well. He asked me if the trial was done and I told him what Harry got.

He's such a nice person! (I mean, Dr. Ross) I believe he really cares. Even Mom thinks he's a nice guy. And you know what? I'm finally getting somewhere with school! I passed all my exams! Yeah! That means that if I pass the next semester, I get to graduate..... as long as these two are born on time, that is.

February 4th

It's 3 a.m. and I can't sleep! These two have been bouncing around like bowling balls hitting the gutters! No matter what position I'm in, nothing is comfortable.

Actually, I woke up from a nightmare. It was really weird.

There I was, standing on the sidewalk, watching a parade go by. But, I wasn't concentrating on the parade. All I could see was this woman and two little boys on the other side of the street. I wanted to go and say hello, but something kept holding me back. She was a pretty woman, not gorgeous, just nice to look at.

Then, Harry came up to her and put his arm around her. He looked up and saw me. I wanted to run and hide! Then the woman got younger and the two kids turned into babies and they were screaming their heads off! Harry yelled at them and then took one in each hand and shook them until their heads fell off! I woke up in a sweat with my heart pounding!

This is really weird!

February 7th

Start of *Festival du Voyageur*. Mom is working volunteer hours at *Festival* at the *Relais du Voyageur* at the Cultural Center. Just so you know, it's a winter festival. See, there's like this tradition in our community.

We host winter games, winter competitions and snow sculpture contests. (That attracts sculptors from as far south as Chili. They come to sculpt snow!) There's also a beard growing contest and the "*Concours du Meilleur*" - that's a contest to determine the best out of the best. That's what the *Voyageurs* used to do. They were young guys that wanted to travel, so they signed up with the Hudson's Bay Company and traveled with a group of explorers, trapped animals, exchanging furs with the aboriginal people for the fur trading company.

The *coureurs de bois* worked for the Northwest Company and were enemies of the voyageurs. Very often they would spur contests between themselves to keep in shape. Do you know that to be a *Voyageur*, you had to be able to lift one hundred and thirty pounds of weight on your back at fourteen or else you weren't hired?

I can't imagine lifting that much weight! That's like.... fifty kilograms. It would take twelve guys from my class four pounds each to compare the weight. I'd need to be an elephant! I'm bad enough as it is, no way am I going to be like an elephant!

And their diet on the road wasn't the greatest.... a cup of dried split peas per person per day.... enough to keep you busy every night!

So, during *Festival* time, my francophone community hosts tourists from as far south as Florida and as far north as the North West Territories and Nunavut. There's contests of all types that mirror what the voyageurs would have done.

For example, there's a race between two people to saw off a log by hand with a bow saw, then another where you work with a partner and saw off another, larger log, with a two-handled saw. The winner then tries to swipe his opponent off a log with a pillow and then as he eliminates all his opponents, he challenges each to '*la jambette*' (that's a leg game).

You lie down on a mat and face each other. Then you each lift up a leg that touches each other. You have to sort of do leg wrestling (instead of hand wrestling) and force your opponent to touch his foot down with your leg. You are flat on your back, you are only allowed to use one leg for the combat and it's a test of strength and strategy.

Then there's the *Shinny*. That's like a hockey game except you're playing with a tennis ball (the pioneers used rolled up gut) and crooked branches. At one end of the branch there's like a curve. Sort of like the end of a hockey stick, except, because it's a branch, it's not curved or flat or straight. It's just plain crooked and at this really weird angle. It's hard to control. Actually, Mr. Adrian (my gym teacher) says that "*Le Shinny*" (pronounced: shee-nee), was the first form of hockey known to man on the North American Continent. It dates back to around 1820! (Or maybe earlier?)

There is a lot to do at *Festival.* There's the Fort where we have a Sugar Shack. In there you'll find hot maple syrup that's poured over a wooden trough filled with fresh snow and then you take a popsicle stick and you roll it over the cooled syrup. It forms a sort of lollipop. You pay two dollars for that and it's really good.

There's also lots of music! Old time fiddling. There are bands from all over the country. Hip hop for the youths at the *Rame de nuit*, and at the *Auberge du Violon,* there's old-fashioned jigging and fiddling to which you can dance to. (It's mostly a hangout for ballroom dancers, but I like it too because the bands are the kind you'd find at a country social.) At the *Grenier de l'Abbaye* there's comedy skits and then at the *Relais des Anciens* (Old-Timers Post), there's skits and plays by the seniors and different villages around Winnipeg.

It's weird that I've lived here all my life and that I never really saw all of this. Winnipeg and St-Boniface are pretty rich in cultural stuff.

Festival lasts nine days and attracts people from all over North America. This year, we're supposed to have Inuit dancers at the opening ceremonies. That should be different!

February 18th

You know what? Moira called! She's setting up appointments for the couples and me to meet. Imagine someone wanting to adopt twins! *Twins!* I wonder what I'll get. Maybe two boys. What would they be like? Harry? Yuk! I sure hope not! Two little horrors that would grow up with his abusive genes. But, I'm giving them up for open adoption. I get to choose who the parents are going to be.

What if its girls? Hmm. Maybe they'll look like me or maybe like Harry or a mix between us. That's a scary thought. My bad habits and Harry's abusive temper. *Oh God!* I hope not! I just hope they won't get parents like the ones I see in my dreams lately. That one about the babies losing their heads is enough to scare anybody!

But what happens if I don't like any of the couples that Moira chooses? What if the only way these two can get adopted is if they are adopted by two couples? What then? How would that come about? I'd have to see more couples or go through another agency. And I always wanted a brother or sister. It wouldn't be fair to these two to be without each other. I'll talk with Moira. Tell her that's not an option for these kids.

February 19th

I hope the parents Optimum Adoption has lined up are going to be really nice. What if none of the applications work out? What if the couples only want babies to have babies, not to raise them up right? What if they only want kids to patch their marriages? That's not a good way to start a family!

I can hear Moira telling me that they screen the potential parents carefully and do home visits for each couple. If there was anything wrong with the reasons the couple wants to adopt, the agency would know and they would hold off an adoption. Wouldn't they?

Moira reminded me that I need to start working on the Openness Agreement Contract. That's how often I'd like to visit these two once they are adopted. She keeps reminding me that it won't be every couple that will agree to have me over to visit once a month or even twice a year. She told me that some couples prefer that I not offer any birthday gifts or christening gifts either.

That got me thinking because it's making me realize how much more important their parents are going to be to them. They'll be the ones to take all the decisions. I won't be there for their first month's birthday or when they get sick or anything like that.

One of the first things Moira explained to Mom and I, was what Open Adoption meant.

She said that a closed adoption was where the birth mother has no further contact with the adoptive parents after the babies are with them. But most importantly, a closed adoption means that I don't choose the parents-to-be. *I can't - couldn't handle that!* These two deserve good parents.

God? Why is it that I'm feeling so uncertain today? So full of questions? It's like there's this big, mean, heavy weight on my shoulders and I don't like it.

Mom calls this 'dumpy-day time'.

Sherry is right in saying that each pregnancy is different. As different and as unique as each mother. Some girls feel grumpy throughout their pregnancy while others are happy as can be.

I'm about two months away from having these babies and I can hardly see my feet in the morning. Mom has to help me put on my boots because I can't see them!

My stomach is like a huge balloon, my back aches almost all the time now and you know what else? I have to go pee almost every hour! Enough that in every one of my classes at school, the teachers have made me switch desks to the one closest to the door and I no longer have a desk like everyone else! It's a table and a chair!

Grumble, grumble. You two better settle down! I'm trying to write here and now I've got wiggly lines all over my page! Wonkabonka!

Cool it, will you? Okay, okay, time to put this diary away for the night. These two are going to keep me awake all night for sure now!

2 a.m.

Told you! I can't sleep. The only thing that might put me to sleep is probably reading over my Chem and Français notes and I don't want to do that. Maybe some ice cream will settle better. Or a hot chocolate. Or just plain chocolate! Now where is that bar I was saving for just a time as this?

February 22nd

I've just come back from another doctor's appointment. Do you know that this month's ultrasound is tomorrow? That's when I'm supposed to do a presentation in Geography class. Instead I've got to be in a hospital room! Mr. Routier isn't going to be very happy about this. I just hope he won't give me a zero! It would be just like him to do that. He is very strict and if we hand in any work late, he takes off thirty points! I need all I can get to graduate!

If Dr. Ross keeps sending me for tests during school hours it's going to be even harder to keep up with my studies. He says that I've lost weight and he's wondering why. *Why?* Well, it wouldn't do if I couldn't get into my clothes would it? And it certainly isn't a good idea to binge like my cravings have wanted me to do.

I read somewhere in a magazine that you can control certain things about your life. Food being one of them. I've got lots of leftover stress from the trial and just two weeks ago, I was pigging out just about every night on caramels with dill pickles or peanut butter with ice-cream, cheese curls and chocolate syrup on top! I was horrified when I weighed myself! I don't want to be bigger than I should be! I'm already having enough problems getting dressed and needing Mom to help with my shoes and boots!

I told Mom that as soon as I finish with the twins and grad that I'm going to get myself a job and help her out with the payments to Legal Aid. She didn't say no.

February 25th

The technician for the ultrasound was frowning during the test. I wonder what's wrong? She and I were chatting about weight and dieting and so on. Sometimes they're fun, but not this time. I mean twenty eight pounds instead of twenty, what's the big deal? I asked Mom why it was important to gain so much weight in a pregnancy and she said it was better for the babies. Frankly, I don't want to cause any grief to these two, but I also want to stop myself from stuffing my face every night when I come back from school. That's not normal! Mom told me I should ask Sherry. My next appointment isn't until next week, so Mom suggested I call her.

Sherry told me that for twins it was important that I put on a bit more weight than for a single child. To remember that I was carrying two lives instead of one. She then said that because I wasn't a very big girl, bone-wise, that twenty eight pounds sounded a bit too much and maybe aim for twenty five or six. I guess she's got a point.

She also said I should talk about it with Dr. Ross. He might have a different reason.

If I divide twenty six by three, no by five.... no that's still not right... twenty five then..... divide by five gives me ten pounds to keep for me and five pounds for each of the babies. Now how is that supposed to make sense? I guess I should ask Dr. Ross why it's important that I gain more weight.

I re-read my last entry and I can't believe I was so EMO! It kind of reminded me of my first trimester. All I did was cry my eyes out at the slightest little thing! Even the guys at school made me crazy!

February 29th

Leap year! We get an extra day. I wonder what happens to the babies that are born on this day. Do they celebrate their birthday on the twenty eighths or the firsts of March? And how about April Fool kids? Gosh! I hope that's not my delivery date!

The guys at school are starting to call me Muscle Lady. I got really mad at Jerry yesterday. He said that he had to be careful of "the little woman because she was pregnant" and he laughed at me with the other guys around him. I saw red and turned on him. Me! Teena Danais! *Me!* The one who used to be so shy! I still can't get over the fact that I stood up to him!

I walked right up to his locker and told him that if he thought I was weak, I was challenging him to a fight. He looked taken aback, but then stared me down and laughed and asked what kind of fight I had in mind. I told him that it would be one that would need all his strength and power and strategy. (He's on the debate team.)

He snickered and laughed loudly and I wasn't sure he was going to take me up on the challenge. His friends taunted him with things like, 'She's pregnant. Winning should be a breeze. You can bet on it.' And 'Teena Danais is a pushover. You'll have no problem.'

I wasn't sure if he'd go for it, but he decided on the spot and said 'Okay. You're on.' Nic took me by the arm and asked me if I was nuts! I chuckled back and said no. I turned to the bully who's been such a jerk to me since I've been in this school and told him to meet me in the cafeteria tomorrow at lunch time. I'd be waiting.

Just you wait Jerry-The-Bully, you're going to get what's coming to you.

March 1st

Today's the day. I'm bringing my secret weapon with me. Oh, I'm going to love this! Mom's on my side and I know that this is going to be a day to remember. *Just you wait Jerry Montcalm.*

6 p.m.

Well, well, well. How the mighty have fallen. The whole class showed up to see the fight! It was really amazing to see Jerry, surrounded by his friends, coming through the door. I met him in the middle of the room. Mrs. B told him that there were rules we needed to know first.

I got a message to go see her this morning before classes. She told me that she'd heard talk in the hallways yesterday and was concerned for me. I told her what I had in mind and she stared at me for a few seconds before bursting into laughter. Then she asked if she could referee "the fight". I laughed with her and agreed.

So... we set up a cardboard wall against a round table and placed the 'tools of the fight' behind it. The table was in the far corner of the room, where no one would see what was behind it. Mrs. B. fixed it with the cafeteria staff that no one would be allowed into the room until she was and that no one was allowed to eat before the fight. She stood 'guard' over the corner until Jerry and I showed up.

Mrs. B gave the rules. They were simple: we couldn't utter a single word; we would need to keep our brains clear and give a good fight with no cheating. We would be frisked before entering the fight arena by two teachers. Mr. R for Jerry and Miss Crock for me. The loser would need to get down on his knees before the victor and accept graciously that he had lost then shake hands. The two parties would then pledge to renounce hurting each other with words or any other means of cruelty after the fight.

If we agreed to these terms, then we had to sign the contract sheet outlining the rules. We both did. M. R frisked Jerry and only came up with a set of house keys, two pens and some change. Mrs. B frisked me and only got my house keys.

You should have heard the noisy gasps when they pulled the cardboard. Jerry opened his mouth to protest, but Mrs. B said: "You agreed and signed Jerry. No going back now." So we both sat down and started.

You know, he's pretty good at Scrabble. But I did win by thirty points! When he got down on his knees and asked me to forgive him for what he'd done and said I sort of didn't see him there. It was as if Harry was kneeling in front of me and asking me to forgive him. I was staring at the floor and he had to ask me again. My throat was so tight I could only nod my head.

When he shook my hand I felt funny inside and my knees weren't too solid either. I wonder why? Didn't Harry make me feel a bit shaky at first too? Is this the same? Am I making a huge mistake thinking that Jerry could be the same way? He's bullied me ever since I've come to this school, why would I expect him to change overnight? Can just one showdown prove anything? *Aaaargh!* I sound like Nic analyzing someone. I'm not the one who wants to be a police profiler.

I'd better get on with my studies. I've got a Physics test next week.

Sherry is right. I sometimes think I'm not as strong as I am. Today has proved her point. I'm no longer afraid to stand up for what I believe in or to stop bullying.

March 10th

Would you believe that the ultrasound says that the babies are crowding themselves and that one of them has moved down? I saw them on the monitor today! Dr. Ross was in the room this time and he and the technician put this belt around my abdomen. I heard their heartbeats! Talk about awesome! Sort of like a whomp, whomp sound instead of the tick tock I expected. Their hands are so small! To think that very soon I'll be delivering them too!

Dr. Ross wants me to book some time at the clinic for the pre-natal birthing coaching. I guess it really is time for that. I asked Sherry if she'd be my coach, but she said my mom would probably be a better choice. Doesn't she like me anymore? Is she mad at me? Is it because I should be acting more grown up? More mature in this decision? Have I disappointed her somehow?

March 11th

I called Sherry because I was upset yesterday. Mom said that
she would understand my feelings and that she would probably
reassure me. She was right, as usual.... Sherry said she wasn't mad or
hurt by anything I've done. She just thought that since Mom recently
helped Laura birth her baby, she'd be a better choice for me. She
reassured me and said she was honored that I had asked her! Now I
have to ask Mom.

March 12th

Passed Physics tests and Chem too. Geography... well there's a
subject I thought I'd like, but it's not at all what I expected. Maybe it
would have been better to take History instead.
Not!
Jerry has been really nice to me lately. When I come to school,
he's been opening the doors for me! Does he feel guilty because I
won?
Nic says that he's not all that bad inside; that he's got really
nice parents and plays jazz piano. We'll just have to wait and see
because I don't trust him. We might have had the Scrabble fight but
he doesn't have to do things for me all the time! Maybe he's only
doing this to get back at me.... Or is he? Maybe he is not all bad
inside. Maybe he's turned over a new leaf as Mrs. B would say. Maybe
he's trying to be nicer instead of bullying or maybe he's trying to...
Guess I'll do like Mom says: 'Give him the benefit of the doubt.'
Mrs. B asked me if I wanted to share what is going on with my
life now with the Français class. She said that I might want to add a
chapter to the talk I gave in English Lit last semester. I told her I'd
think about it.

March 15th

So much has happened at school in the last few days that I
hardly had a spare minute to write about the adoption! I met two of
the couples. They're nice, but there's something missing. I don't know,
it's as if there's a wall between me and them, sort of like a drape or

something. Sometimes I feel as if there's no sound going from me to them either. REALLY weird!

The Sheridans brought family photos, but there's still.... I don't know. They've got everything I asked for but it's difficult talking to them.

The Comptes are .... nice, I suppose, but they didn't have family pictures. They just sat there with their heads down and when Moira asked them what they had done after church the last Sunday; Mr. Compte said that they didn't go very often.

I looked at Moira and she winked at me. I guess she got the message. These two deserve more than I. They deserve parents that are involved in their Christian community.

They'll need that foundation to be able to be well-rounded citizens. I don't want them to make the same mistakes I've done. Look what happened with Charlotte! If I had had two parents who believed in God and lived by the right principles of life, I'm sure that she wouldn't have been as attractive as she was to me. I'm sure that if I'd had a father growing up, I could have talked to him and it would have made the difference. Maybe he would have seen that Harry wasn't the right guy for me.

Plus, having two parents would have been a huge weight off Mom's shoulders.

March 14th

The Barnabes have to be it! They're the second to last couple! Moira said that sometimes what we think we want for our babies isn't always the case. I asked what she meant by that and she said that just like I had said the Comptes would be a good couple, that I had been disappointed, hadn't I? Our time together was up and she asked me to think about that and that she was going to set up an appointment with the couple soon.

She's got a point.

What if there aren't any couples that will adopt these two? Does that mean I'm stuck with them?

Oh my! Brain freeze!

March 17th

I wish I could say that the Barnabes are the ones, but they didn't pass with flying colors either. They're a lot older than I thought for one thing. They've been married for twelve years! What if I have to choose one of these couples? What if I have to take second best? Would that be a good idea?

What if they aren't the best choice? What if it would be the worst thing I could do? These two deserve the best! They deserve more than I can give them, more than I can provide for them now. *Oh, my two little ones! I want more than anything that you would have a family and parents that will love you for who you are, for what you can be and more importantly that will give you their hearts to love in return for your love.*

I only wish I had the stamina, the strength of character and courage to keep you, but I don't. I know I can't be your mother. I'm not good with children.

I failed with Monster and all the others didn't I? Why would this be any different? I know that finishing High School is important, that keeping a baby or babies with the birth mother is important too, but I can't find it in me to do this.

I can't! I just can't! It hurts my very soul just thinking about this. I just wish I didn't have to sit on this fence top. I even wish I'd never, ever met Harry, given in to him or gone out with him!

March 18th

Dr. Ross says that I might not make it to term. He says that with twins there is always a likelihood of an early birth or a difficult one. He said that he'll let me know when he wants me in the hospital. When I asked him why he was so concerned, he just said that everything looked good, but that it was better to be prepared than caught off-guard. I told him we started the birthing classes and he asked me who my coach was.

I told him it was Mom and his eyes crinkled at the sides and he said that was a very good choice. I laughed too. Well, Sherry wasn't going to, so what choice did I really have? Plus, Mom's already been a birthing coach, so to a certain extent that made the decision easier for me.

You know, I think Mom and Dr. Ross would be good for each other. He's so nice! And so is she.

March 20th

Moira tackled me tonight. She asked me if I had finally written that letter called 'Birth Mother's Letter'. I just don't feel like it! If I write the letter, it feels as if these two would belong to me and be attached to me somehow. Well, they are, but, they're... you know.... just babies, not anyone I really know.

When I said that to her, she smiled sort of weird but firm. "You need to write it. It's not an option. Think in the long run instead of just now. Think about the twins when they start asking their parents where they came from. Ask yourself if you think they won't be angry with you for giving them their parents instead of you taking them as their mother because you were too involved with yourself or that you hated them."

That had me stop in my tracks. I don't want these two to ever, EVER think I'm giving them to good parents because I hate them! I realize that I'm too young to raise them how they need to be raised. I don't want them to feel that I'm just passing them on like cabbage leaves to a compost bin.

What else is there to do? Just in case I lose my nerve, here's my first and last draft:

"Dear twins,

It's hard for me to write this because you are still in the womb, still in your little house. Throughout these months, I've questioned my decision to give you to good, loving parents. You see, I'm too young to keep you. My mother (your grand-mother) had me when she was young and she never married because she was too afraid to have a man hurt me like she was hurt.

I was hurt too, but I want you to know what it is to have a good father. I missed having someone like a man to teach me what a father was like, to hug me when I was down or hurting. I'd really like to try to be a good mother, but I know deep down that I'm not going to be able to make the grade.

You two deserve the best and I can't give it to you. I have heard that twins have a special bond. I pray that God will create and foster that bond between the two of you, because you deserve each other.

You deserve the best that love can give.

In fact, that's why I'm giving you away.

I'm giving you the opportunities that I never had. The chance of a stable home, one where there are two parents, standing side by side, worrying about the two of you side by side and praying for you side by side.

Whatever you decide to do with your lives, know that I will always think of you and every night when I look up in the sky and see the twin constellation, I'll whisper a prayer of safekeeping over you."

I feel strange now. As though something in my heart has shifted. Am I really a mom? No. I'm a soon to be ex-mother. And I don't think that signing the letter as 'Your mom' is appropriate. I'll have to ask Sherry what I should write. I don't think asking Moira is a good idea. She'd be horrified that I didn't care.

It's not that I don't care. It's just that these two aren't mine. I'm not their mother, I'm just the carrier.

March 21st

I re-read that letter and I've decided that I wasn't being very honest with myself or the babies. In fact, I wrote a very selfish letter. In a way I do love them, just not like a mother should. So I'm changing a few things like:

'Don't think that I don't love you. I do. Quite a lot, but it wouldn't be right to keep you when I know I'm not mature enough to take care of you properly.' And where I talk about the stars at night: 'know that I will always love you from afar and every night when I look up in the sky, I'll whisper a prayer of safekeeping over you. Love,' and I'll just sign my name.

March 22nd

Tonight I met THE couple. The ones that will be their parents. It's a strange feeling. Like knowing that you've come home or that you're stepping into a warm hug. Let me tell you about them.

Mrs. Colliers is petite. She's got straight brown hair to her shoulders and the most intense blue eyes I've ever seen. Mr. Colliers is tall, dark haired and he looks at his wife like she's the most precious thing in the world. They shared that they have a little nephew of three that they've baby-sat over the past year. Mr. Colliers showed me a photo and he looks so sweet and innocent.

They also had a photo album, different from the others. For one thing, Mrs. Colliers is quite an artist. She scrapbooked their life. Just for me! There was their meeting at the park, their engagement and wedding plus other weddings in their families. Everyone was smiling.

Then there were two pictures that stole my breath!

One was of a small baby. So tiny that it looked almost like a doll. I thought that they didn't have any other children and when I looked up at them, Mr. Collier had his arm around his wife and she had tears in her eyes. He said that it was their son.

The caption beside the photo said that it was Nathan, born early at twelve weeks premature.

Next to the picture lay a little golden cross that touched the edge of the second photograph of a sandy beach where a verse from Psalms was written neatly. "Yeah, though I walk through the shadow of the valley of death, I will fear no evil, for my Lord is my staff and my strength. Whom shall I fear?"

It hit me that this couple is not afraid to share their trials and heartaches. The Colliers are soft spoken and gentle of spirit and they not only smile through their tears, but they are willing to take a chance on a girl who is having a hard time with two babies! Neither are they judgmental about how I got pregnant!

Moira asked me if I had something to share with them and I felt really dumb because I hadn't got such a nice album myself. When I said I was sorry that it wasn't as nice as Mrs. Colliers, she said that scrapbooking the album had helped her grieve the death of their dreams to have more children. Little Nathan hadn't lived for more than a few hours.

She said that she couldn't have any more children and that the sacrifice that I was doing was more than they could ever have hoped for. I had tears in my eyes!

Moira said that she would give us both a chance to think things over for a day or two. I guess that's wise, because this couple is really special. They deserve the best.

March 28th

I'm at the hospital for another of those pesky ultrasounds! I've got to go pee and I can't! I'm trying to keep my mind off the discomfort studying for exams next week. This is Spring Break and I hope that I pass my Physics course.

March 30th

I met with Moira today. She asked me when my doctor thinks that I'll deliver the babies. I told her what he told me a little while ago and she said that was okay, just to let her know when I went into labor.

Then she asked me what I had thought of the Colliers. I told her that they were the ones I'd picked. She said she agreed with me. Now, she asked me who will be naming these babies - me or the Colliers. I asked her if it was okay to meet with them again so that we could get to know each other better. She said she'd see and get back to me.

April 2nd

Would you believe I'm only a few weeks before I have these two? School is getting to be difficult. Mrs. B and the counselors are putting a home study program together for me so that I can graduate with the rest of my class. As it is, I'm tired all the time and I'm finding it really hard to concentrate in class with these two kids jousting in there. My lower back hurts sometimes and my abdomen can barely fit under the table top. In fact I think that it would probably lift the whole thing up a good half foot!

Moira, Mom and I are meeting the Colliers tomorrow at their home. I wonder what it looks like?

April 3rd

Their house is older than ours, in fact almost as old as the house next door. Mrs. Colliers asked that I call her Carolyn if I didn't mind her calling me Christina. I said it was okay, but that I preferred Teena. She said that she loved my real name and that it reminded her of her courageous Christ. I had never thought of my name as being Christ like, but she's right!

She said that she and Don, her husband, had talked it over and wondered if I wouldn't mind giving the middle names of the babies. I asked her why she would want me to name the children that will be hers and her husband's. Here's what she said: "You are the one that has nourished them with health and wise decisions throughout their most important growth time. You deserve that right."

They are something else these people! *God? Thank you for these two people. They are from Your will in my life. Thank You that You brought them into mine.*

Mom says that if she had had parents like them, she might never have left her village or been rebellious and gotten into a pack of lies and trouble and hurt.

Carolyn said that if I wanted to, I could nurse the babies after they were born. I said that I hadn't thought about it and that if she wanted me to, I guess I could, but then I asked her if she didn't want to herself. Her eyes got all misty and she smiled! She smiled!

Wow! It was like a rainbow stretching across the room! How can she smile after what she's gone through? Remember the picture of Nathan? He wasn't their only child. Carolyn had three other miscarriages after he was born! She's still smiling! That almost makes me look like a selfish brat who thinks the world is all made of roses and gold platters.

I still can't get over the fact that Don and Carolyn are so positive!

April 12th

Well.... two weeks to go. Dr. Ross says that I need to start thinking about getting out of school and get lots of rest periods. He says that one of the twins has turned and that means I'm close.... *Close!* I called Moira and Sherry and told them that.

Carolyn and Don said they'll supply the car seats and diaper bag for the babies when Moira comes to pick them up. It's amazing that I can even think positively now about this whole process.

It's been tough lately, with all the appointments of match meetings, working on the 'Intent To Place' document. That's the document where I name the adoptive parents. They have to fill one out called the 'Intent To Receive'. It's a pretty complicated process.

Remember that twenty one day clause? The one I wasn't sure about? I was pretty confused and I thought that it was the clause that said that I got to keep these two for the 21 days after they were born and then handed them over. But that's not it.

These two will be given over to their new parents forty eight hours after they are born as long as the doctors let them go and then I have twenty one days to think about them being with their adoptive parents. I could take them out of their arms! But I couldn't do that to Carolyn and Don! They are just the right people for these two!

April 14th

I re-wrote my Birth Mother's Letter. Now that I know Don and Carolyn, I know what to write. I've kept the opening sentences and added these:

"Your parents are very special people. Carolyn has the heart of a lioness. One that protects those she loves. She has a way of talking that gives me goose bumps because she feels what I feel, she thinks how I think and she acts the way I would like to act.

Don is calm and in control but not in a controlling way. He's a stronghold. Like a beacon in the night when you're lost. He doesn't speak a lot but what he says is always right on the ball and always with a heart of deep seated faith. I like that about him. He's a person that I'd like to have had as a father.

I want you to know, the both of you, that I will always love you. No matter what. I also want you to know that I was too young to be a good enough parent. Carolyn and Don will be and are your true parents. They have yearned for you and loved you even before you were born.

And always remember that God is the one who has made this blessing possible. Rely on Him for all your needs. No matter what they are. He'll always be there for you; to listen to you and to comfort you. When I'll look up into the darkness of night, I'll search for the Twin constellation and think of you, send you my blessing and love. May your lives be enriched by the two people who loved enough to accept me as I was and greet and love you as their own. Your biological mother."

Well, I guess that was more than two or three sentences. But at least, it's here in this diary. If ever I need to come back to this point in my life, at least the words will help me remember the reason why I took this decision.

April 16th

Remember the form that Harry had to sign? The "Notice To Birth Father"? Moira finally got it back from him. He's given up his rights to claim these two as his! Thank goodness it came before their birth!

April 20th

I had this horrible pain in my back today and it's just hard moving around. It's like this vice around my lower body. Really weird!

April 21st

I think I'm in labor! My water broke and I'm wet through! Ow! Ow! Ow!!!! Really strong contractions! Mom is getting the- *oooh!*
Sorry... you know... I think I'm going to pick up the thread in a few... days... *Gotta go! These two are in a hurry to be born! God HELP!!!*

April 22nd

My throat is raw from grunting to push them out! It was a tough time, but I survived! I'm just so tired! No energy whatsoever!

April 23rd

Today, I have to say good-bye to these two beautiful babies! Two little boys. They don't look like Harry. More like Mom and I and the most amazing thing is that they each have a dimple like Don when they smile!
I get to give them their middle names. Twin 1 is forevermore Ryan and twin 2 is Raylend. I don't know why, just that, when I look at them, that's what comes to my mind. It's almost as if God is giving

me their names. I feel so blessed that I had this time to connect with them.

Raylend's toes curl when he feeds, while Ryan's fingers grab my long hair. I had never thought that each would have his own personality, but they do. I'm doing the right thing. Carolyn and Don are the perfect parents to love them both. I can't wait to have the blessing of transfer ceremony.

I'm expressing my milk with a special pump that the nurse practitioner passed me. She said that it is better for the babies to receive the birth mother's milk for a few days that it will help them fight off diseases. I agreed, so that's what I'm doing, but I have to admit it's not very comfortable or easy. Dr. Ross came to see me this morning and said that he'd prescribe some medication to help the milk dry out once I left the hospital.

Carolyn and Don are going to have the chore of feeding the two suckers (they feed every two to three hours!) with the expressed milk then they'll switch to formula mixed in with it. I think Carolyn has the right to feed them. She's the real mom. I'm the in-between one now.

The Colliers have invited us to the ceremony that will be held with Moira, their pastor, them and us in their home in three days time. It will be at this private ceremony that they'll have them dedicated to the Lord too. A special time. One that I wouldn't miss for the world!

April 24th

I didn't expect to cry like this! I miss them already! Why did I agree to this? I feel awful! If it wasn't for Mom and Moira, I'd be on my way to see Carolyn and Don right now to pick them up and bring them home! Why did I agree? Why? *Why?*

10 p.m.

I shouldn't have written that up there. I should have crossed it out or whited-it out. I know I'm doing this for the two of them, not for me. They deserve better than what I can give them, better than what I can offer them and better parents. Actually two parents who will raise and watch over them better than what I ever could.

April 26th

Mom and I talked about the fact that I was taking the
chance of her being a grandmother out of her hands. I wanted her
to understand that I hadn't chosen to hurt her on purpose. She told
me that she wasn't offended and that the decision had been mine to
make, not hers and that she was very proud of me and what I had
accomplished so far. She also told me that she found me very brave
and she loved me more than ever! It's nice to know that I haven't hurt
her.

In a few hours Mom and I will head over to the Colliers. I'm
hoping I won't burst into tears and spoil the night for them. Ryan
and Raylend deserve to have this evening as their new beginning.
Yesterday I thought that maybe I can go back to school next week.
Now I think I'd better wait another week. See how I am after tonight.

April 27th

The Colliers were so.... oh, I can't explain it. So in love, I guess,
with the two of them. Carolyn glows when she holds them. Don
didn't stop chattering about their progress. I think he carries a tape
measure in his pocket so he can measure their length - head to toe
- every half hour. ;-) At the ceremony, their pastor prayed from the
heart.

I can understand now why the Colliers are such special people.
They take God's word to heart in everything they do. It's not just
show. It shines from them in every aspect of their behavior. I couldn't
have picked better. When we got there, Carolyn invited me to go
upstairs with her to the nursery.

It's pretty in there. The boys have separate beds and have a
mobile over each of them. She gave me the choice of either having
only one in my arms or both. We looked at each other and it was like
she knew before I even said anything that I needed both in my arms.
I cuddled them a bit, but already I felt as if they didn't belong to me.
Like they craved Carolyn's loving touch.

Ryan was fussing and Raylend screwed his face up to cry. By
the time we got to the lighting of the candles, Raylend was crying. I
passed him over first. It was like magic!

Their pastor said that this younger by a minute brother was Luke. He would be the treasure. As soon as Carolyn took him in her arms, Luke Raylend stopped crying and smiled up at her. Mom looked at me at the same I did at her! We both knew that my decision had been the right one.

Then it was Ryan's turn. The pastor said that this firstborn was to be Christopher. He would be a leader. When Don took him, the baby fit neatly into his hand and arm. Christopher quieted right down. Mom and I had tears running down our faces. Carolyn and Don were just as bad.

With the openness contact agreement, I know I'll see these two in a little while. Carolyn promised to send me photos in a few months. Before we left their home, she gave me one of the candles she had prepared for tonight. "Remember that we will always love you because you have made us complete. We will honor the treasures that you have given us and raise them up to be like you. Courageous and positive."

I know I've done the right thing. Things will work out fine now.

April 30th

Moira was right when she said that I'd have a tough time with letting them go. It is tough, but at the same time I know that the decision I made is right for the boys. I still cry at home and sometimes it hurts to see the mothers in the park playing with their children, but then I see a young mother, almost my age, screaming at her kids and I think to myself that Christopher and Luke will never have me yelling at them or having me turn my anger against them. They'll be nourished and treated with love and affection. And I know Don will guide them in the way they need to go.

I'm going back to school next week. It's time. If I stay home I'm going to be really hiding. I need my friends and I need to stay busy.

May 11th

I know it's been a while, but I didn't really want to talk to anyone, not even write in my diary. There are a lot of memories here.

They hurt and I'm scared of remembering. There have been a lot of things going on. Sherry called to set-up an appointment, but I didn't feel like talking to her or even Moira. Mom tried too, but I just didn't feel like talking.

I saw Dr. Ross today and he asked me the same thing. "You miss them, don't you?"

I'm ashamed to say that I do, but I said that I was confused because I know they are where they need to be.

"It's okay to be upset and sad, Teena. That's the normal process of grieving. Talking about it will help."

I don't know what to do! I hurt bad!

May 12th

Mrs. B picked up on it at school today and asked me if there was anything she could do to help.

I started crying and she just hugged me and told me she understood what I was feeling. When I told her she couldn't even start to understand what was going on with me, she stepped back and led me to her classroom. She sat me down and told me why my speech earlier in the year had so impressed her.

Mrs. B. not only got pregnant when she was my age, but she also made a decision that affected the rest of her life. I thought then that she was going to tell me she kept her baby. But no, she had an abortion. She told me that she listened to wrong counsel and she still lives with regrets.

"That act of cowardliness on my part tainted many of my relationships with men over the years."

I asked her if she still felt like that. She smiled sadly and said that although she eventually got married and has children of her own now, that it was very difficult for many years because she blamed herself for her choice and she mostly realized that she had killed a human child, kept him or her from having good parents.

"I had nightmares for months after the procedure." She also had feelings of helplessness. She had difficulty just staying in any type of relationship. "I felt lost and sad. I ran away from the situation instead of facing it like you did."

But mostly what I heard was how she was having trouble forgiving herself. I asked her that and she looked at me.

"How can I forgive myself? I'm the one that took that decision. I'm the one that killed."

Suddenly I felt as if I was standing in a courtroom. It was weird that I saw myself as the guilty party; I felt like Mrs. B instead. The judge frowning at her and telling her that she had killed her child. It brought back my reasons for not taking the 'morning after pill' and then I was back in the present, seeing the guilt all over Mrs. B's face.

I put my hand over hers and told her about God and how He loves me, warts and all. How he loves her too. Then I told her about the Colliers and what they were like and how we just connected spiritually over a few minutes of getting to know each other.

It is really strange that I was the one offering comfort to someone who is older than me.

God? What is it that You want me to do with my life? If Mrs. B regrets like this, if she is hurting like this, what can I do to help her? Are there other people, women and men that don't know that their lives can be healed by You?

This is really.... different.... strange.... yet wonderful and amazing. It's like God is trying to tell me something important and I'm just not hearing it or maybe I'm resisting?

I'm tired Lord. Please, can we get back to this tomorrow? There's a whole bunch of things to do for grad and I've got some catching up to do if I want to graduate.

May 14th

I saw Moira today. We had an interesting conversation. She says that I'm a fast healer. When I asked her why she thinks so, she explained that usually most birth mothers take up to a year to heal after giving up their children. She says I'm way ahead of them.

I smiled at that and told her that God being in my life helps me a lot. I'm reading my Bible every morning and working hard at school work and getting my life on track. She asked me what I was thinking of doing after graduation.

It told her God had something very special lined up for me, but that I didn't know yet what it was. She shook her head and told me that it sounded more like I hadn't decided if I wanted to work or go to university.

I shook my head and told her that she had it all wrong, but that I could understand why she would think that. Anyway, without going into the whole session, we agreed to see each other a couple more times. I'm seeing Sherry tomorrow. I hope that she'll help me see what God has for me.

May 15th

I'm glad I went to see her. Sherry agreed with me that I'm progressing well, though she warned me that I might be sad some days and that eventually the sadness would settle into a comfort knowing my two boys were where they were best. She said that I was reassured now by the knowledge that my boys were with good parents and that I knew that I had made the decision based on my beliefs and with the knowledge that I knew what I could and couldn't do, that I knew my limits.

When I told her what had happened with Mrs. B. she smiled sadly and told me that women that have an abortion sometimes hemorrhage very badly after it. They sometimes die too. She said that some abortions can cause later problems with getting pregnant and that many women have serious health repercussions, such as infections, miscarriages, breast cancer risks or that sometimes an abortion misses a pregnancy in the fallopian tubes.

She asked me how I was doing at school and I told her of seeing the children at the playground at the park behind it on my way home every day. She asked if this was a constant reminder of what I had lost. I told her no, because it reinforces my reasons for getting Christopher and Luke adopted.

Then we discussed my future. I told her what God has been trying to tell me and I asked her for her insights. We prayed and I think I've a better idea now.

I'm a lot calmer than I've been with this. Tomorrow, I think I'll go talk with Mrs. B. about the idea that came through after Sherry and I prayed together. Tonight, I'm going to run it by Mom.

10 p.m.

Mom thought my idea was great and suggested I go speak to the school counselors to see what sort of courses would help me.

May 20th

We'll be heading into exams in two weeks. I'm hoping that all the hard work of catching up will be enough. I've passed all the tests and I've handed in all the lab work and projects they gave me. Now all I can do is wait and hope.

But first there's the Fashion Show. I put my name in to model..... I hope I get in. I've almost lost all the weight I gained during the pregnancy and my abdomen is almost as flat as what it was before.

5 p.m.

There was a letter in the mail box. Inside, a picture of Chris and Luke. They are doing well and they are gaining weight. Carolyn wrote that she was wondering if I'd like to have a grad party at their place in early July to celebrate my last year of school. I think I'd like that.

10 p.m.

I talked it over with Mom. She said we'll need to think it over first and talk to Carolyn and Don. Neither one of us wants to impose.

June 4th

Exams! And you know what else? I've lost all the weight I gained with the pregnancy and I'm going to be part of the fashion show! I'm a model! Only three more weeks before Grad! I hope I pass!

June 10th

Well, that's done and over with! I spoke with Mrs. B about my idea and she squealed and hugged me! She said it was a great idea and that she'll be pleased to help put it together. She also said that she'd be really interested in going with me to see the school director. I'm hoping he'll go for it.

I'll tell you about the idea later. I've got to put this in prayer because it's going to rock the school... or schools? Soon. *Very soon....*

June 13th

The fashion show is a fund-raiser for Grad. There is a theme every year and we put together music, lighting, choreography and lots of hard work to make it good.

This year the theme is Fashion in Bloom so we've got flower pots at each end of the stage and there are flowers on most of the clothes we get to model. There's casual and sport and career and formal evening. Of course, we finish with formal evening and I love my gown!

Mark's mom is a florist and she's put together fourteen... no sixteen hand tied bouquets of silk flowers for us. Mrs. N and Mr. D have put the show together and they're going to helps us with the choreography.

We'll be selling tickets for the show and the home-ec class is baking cakes and cookies for a bake sale at intermission.

We're going to hold it in the gym and I'm really looking forward to seeing Mom there.

Hey! I forgot to tell you. Remember Dr. Ross? He and Mom really hit it off when I delivered Chris and Luke! They've been dating for almost a month now. That is so awesome!

June 16th

Show time! I'll tell you later!

June 17th

Last night was awesome! We had a great time! I think I forgot to mention that all the clothes we wore were loaners? My gown came from a bridal shop and it has these beautiful blue flowers from the edge of the collar to the hem of the dress. I fell in love with it and I'd love to wear it to Grad, but I know Mom can't afford it. Neither can I so I'll just be wearing my Sunday dress to Grad. At the supper, Nic is wearing a long dress but I'll wear the same dress.

I know that just about everybody else is going to wear a long dress and I know that I should be feeling the pressure to be like everybody else, but I don't.

If there is one thing that this year has taught me it's that I am a valuable person. I have rights and ideas and integrity.

I made a decision that was right for Christina Marie Danais and right for Chris and Luke. I have a head that can think and make decisions with wise counsel.

So what if I'm not like others? If I stood against the walls and felt sorry for myself all the time, I wouldn't be alive. I'd be in a deep depression and that's not an option.

Sherry is right. I am courageous and I know what God has in line for me. I'm going to be a teacher. Maybe a counselor. (I'll have to see later.)

This time next week, I'll be on my own. I spoke with Moira and she's essentially discharged me from her care. She says that my 'idea' is great and she wishes me good success. She said that I can come back and talk with her whenever I have issues, but she said that she didn't think I'd need to.

"Through this experience, you've grown strong Teena. Continue to be strong. I know you'll be a fine woman."

I know where my boys are. I know they are with people that love them and when I see them on the 1st of July, I'll be even more certain. Instead of having a grad party, Mom and I thought that celebrating a national holiday might be better. I'm not sure Carolyn is going to listen though. She sounded sort of mysterious last time she called Mom. Something's brewing...

June 20th

I was never so shocked in my life! My class has named me Valedictorian! We all had votes to cast and because this is a fair society school (democratic, some say) there is a female and male Valedictorian. Guess who is my partner? Jerry Montcalm! Seems he's learnt an important lesson this year. *Humility!*

Mrs. B. is helping me with my speech and I hope it will go over well.

June 25th

Grad! Twelve years plus one, if you count Kindergarten, done and over with! You'd think that I'd feel different? Well, I guess I do.

Now starts a new life. One that will take a lot of courage and love.

I'm putting my speech between the pages here because it is too long to write in here. I'll just quote something from it.

"We leave our youth behind us, not to be forgotten, but to be used as a foundation upon which we can continue to build. We aim for adulthood. A path that will lead us towards a career for some, a trade for others, but certainly towards a good life serving in the best of our capacity our society and community."

Jerry's speech talked about the lessons we learned throughout the school years. You know which one impressed me the most? Here it is, and I quote:

"We sometimes think, growing up, that winning every battle is the important thing. Battles are fought and won in many different ways.

Fighting can only be done if it is done fairly, never in a way that crushes another person. If we fight, we need to know what and why we are fighting. Like our parents fought to keep French in our schools. Our duty is to continue to fight to keep that language alive and to fight for our freedoms and what we believe in."

Then he went on to thank our teachers for their patience and guidance. But you know what floored me?

He asked me to be his escort for the grad dinner! You know where? In front of everyone in the audience! He got down on one knee and took a red rose out from behind his back and presented it to me right there and then! If my heart hadn't melted when he first asked my forgiveness back when we had that Scrabble fight, I think that the tears that ran down my face this time were genuine. I couldn't refuse in front of my class and I couldn't refuse when I looked into his eyes. My heart melted and I accepted his rose.

Our class rose to their feet and so did the audience. They applauded and Jerry got red as a beet! That's when we looked at each other and started laughing so hard we both had trouble getting off the stage!

June 29th

Grad dinner tonight! Mom had a surprise for me. She and Dr. Ross took me shopping yesterday evening. Shopping! He's a real sweetheart and the way he looks at Mom is kind of scary. I mean not scary, scary, but in a .... .hmmmm.... it's kind of like she goes all gooey inside...I think they're in love! Wouldn't it be awesome if they got married? She'd be happy at last and *I'd have a Dad! Wow!*

11 p.m.

I'm home! What a night! Jerry is so nice! He's a lot different than I thought. And he's a real gentleman. Nothing like Harry and nothing like what I thought he was. He's going to university this fall. He's going to be studying to be a chiropractor, like his Dad. The amazing thing is that we get on well together.

I had a bit of difficulty dancing with him, but, he told me that he respected me enough to let me put the boundaries I needed.

He asked me out again and I said I'd think about it. Both he and I didn't want to go to Safe Grad, so we ended up going for soft drinks at the donut shop with Nic and her escort. It was a nice ending to the night.

It is strange that now that I'm on my own, out of school that I've got tears rolling down my cheeks. It's not that I miss anyone, only that I realize that I've closed a chapter of my life!

I've grown so much over the last year that I wonder if I'm eighteen or if in reality I'm thirty? Tonight I felt a little bit out of place sometimes and it was an eye opener. Eva and her gang were giggling over silly stories and Doug and his gang pulled stupid pranks and jostled those around them at the dinner and dance. They are so babyish and immature, it made me sick!

I almost forgot to tell you that when Mom and Dr. Ross took me shopping they bought me the dress I modeled for the show! It's mine! And you know what Mom said?

"You, my daughter Christina, deserve this gift. You've worked so hard since April to get where you are now. I'm so proud of you."

July 1st

I get to see Chris and Luke today! Yeah!

Midnight

Well, we're back. Mom and I and Dean (that's Dr. Ross) went to see my babies. They've grown!

They are so healthy and they smile a lot!

Carolyn and Don had a cake that said *Congrats!* on it and Mom and Dean gave me earrings. I should have known the four of them had planned this! The boys gave me a bookmark for my Bible and a special highlighter for Bible study.

Their thoughtfulness really warmed my heart. We then went to watch the fireworks and came home.

I got to hold my two boys in my arms again, but I didn't feel anything in particular; only that of a family friend holding someone's baby. It's interesting to realize that I don't miss them as much as I thought I would. Not that it means that I don't love them; I'm not like a water tap that has been turned off! Rather, I know they are where they belong and that in a nutshell is what God has done for me.

Tonight, when Don asked me what I was thinking of doing now, I shared the IDEA with everyone. Here it is:

God gave me a verse that illustrates what I want to do with the rest of my life.

"You shall love your neighbor as yourself. There is no other commandment greater than these."

The verse prior to that one talks about loving God and honoring and adoring only one God. That's from Mark chapter 12, verse 31. If we do not want others to suffer as we do, we love them more than ourselves.

I want to live to be an example of love to other teens that need to hear about the dangers of infatuation. About the dangers of unsolicited sex. About the danger signs of date rape, of abortion, of making the right decisions for their lives.

After talking it over with Mrs. B, the school director and counselors, I will be taking specialized courses at the university on counseling and teaching. They've also encouraged me to prepare a short presentation as a run-through for them.

I'll be meeting with them in early August. Here are a few guidelines that I'm going to stick to:

- Many boys and young men haven't any idea how their actions and anger can transform them. If Harry had gotten the help he needed, maybe he wouldn't have assaulted me. If I can help just one young man turn away from the tempting deceit of sexual power, I'll guide a lost soul to find purity of heart.
- Help young people change their views of what it means to remain pure for the helpmate God has set aside for them and maybe help our world become one without AIDS or social diseases.
- If I can reach just one girl to steer her away from an abusive relationship, then I'll have answered God's calling and His purpose for my life.

Adoption is an option of love.
It completes those who wait;
Those who long for a 'little one' to love and guide;
It gives them a chance at Living.

Acknowledgments

Thank you to Helen H, Lynda D, Marlene and Becky, Chad, Janique, Keith E, France, Lori and Elysa. You all helped make this story credible and were there when I needed you most.

My heartfelt thanks go out to the Winnipeg Police Service (several departments and friends) for their guidance and patience answering *all* my questions. R. West and Tony F. for legal advice. Adoption Options for open adoption procedures. Claire N (Baby Think It Over program). The too-many-to-name school, family counselors and psychologists for their insights. The Family Crisis Centre for their support, ideas and kindness.

All adoption documentation is taken from the 'Manitoba Adoptions Act'.

LaVergne, TN USA
04 May 2010

181510LV00001B/247/P